To my daughter Jaymie.
Thank you for being such an inspiration.
Thank you for being you.

Evil and hate dwell within; jealousy and envy prevail. Betrayal and trickery overrule where love appears to fail. A wicked serpent shall curse the land and leave his darkened mark. Salvation reveals one frail of flesh but with a mighty heart. The curse will turn these lands to black with dismal hue. Two kings shall pass; a queen shall reign and have to start anew. Courage and kindness are the mark of the Golden Creature to emerge. And from these lands, at last, the vile curse shall finally be purged.

—The Maasakai Kingdom Prophecy

I AWAKENED FROM a horrendous dream into a ghastly reality, my mind cloudy and heavy from the night before. Amarula, oh my goodness, the nectar of the gods. I remember sitting around the fire, drinking glass after glass. When I got up to use the bathroom, I stumbled a little and thought back to earlier in the day when our guide told us about the marula tree and its hard, little, yellowish-brown fruits. Christiaan went on to tell us the fruit ferments and becomes intoxicating. He explained that the animals find the sweet, succulent fruit irresistible, and they gorge themselves on the flesh and the fruit until they, too, become intoxicated. In particular, the monkeys eat so much and become so drunk that they fall out of the trees onto the ground below. In my own intoxicated state, I giggled.

"I'm a little monkey; I'm a little monkey," I murmured in a singsong voice on my way to the ladies' room.

But later, with the pounding headache and stomach bile threatening to let loose at any moment—I was no longer finding it funny. The I'm-a-little-monkey chant got all mixed up with a shrieking that sounded both near and far away at the same time.

"She's gone! She's gone!" repeated over and over, my mind so befuddled I couldn't tell if I was dreaming or if someone was, indeed, screaming. No matter, either way, my thumping head retaliated in agony.

Soon there came a banging on the door, more like the shutters that served as a pseudobarrier between the rest of the world and me.

"Madam, madam, come please," the voice begged.

I rolled out of bed, struggling to stand upright.

Where the hell is David?

The throbbing in my head had become only more intense as the moments ticked by. I could barely keep my stomach contents contained within my body. I staggered to the door in my flimsy pajamas. As I approached, the pounding on the shutters became only more insistent.

"What IS it?" I hissed as I pushed open the doors.

Akilah gasped, "Madam, Little Miss is gone!"

YOU WOULD HAVE THOUGHT I'd be excited about this opportunity to visit Africa, but it was quite the opposite. David had it in his mind that because he had landed this vital assignment, Hannah and I should go with him. He had been asked to do an expose on the historic conditions and peril of Africa's Big Five, but it was unclear to me why he insisted we come along.

My first reaction was, "No. Now is not the time."

I had so much going on, and the thought of preparing our family for that kind of trip was far too daunting. The fact that we were going to have to pull our daughter out of her expensive school for this significant amount of time seemed ridiculous to me, simply outlandish. I came up with a million reasons why this was a bad idea, but I knew it was all futile. He would win; we would go no matter how much I protested. Whatever David wants, David gets.

When did I become so boring? There had been a time when I would have given anything to undertake such an adventure—preparation be damned. I caught a glimpse of myself in the mirror. *Oh man, there she is: an old, boring drunk.*

I'd become a miserable excuse for a mom and an even more miserable woman. At least when I played with Hannah, I made an effort. I tried to be fun, within certain parameters, of course. Our fun couldn't make too much of a mess because I'd have to clean it up. It, for sure, had to be safe. And it had to be easy. No complications for this mom. If it wasn't easy and it required too much effort, it wasn't happening. I felt so damn tired all the time, just thinking about doing things exhausted me.

Oh wow. What have I become? I felt like I was no longer

recognizable to myself. I checked the mirror again. *Nope, nobody there that I recognize.*

I moved from the hall into the kitchen. Without a moment's hesitation, I reached for the cabinet door, the one that is closest to the refrigerator, the one that contained my relief. I reached for the bottle. It slid off the shelf with a satisfying sound, but I quickly realized it only had a sip or two left. Damn it, not nearly enough. I padded out to the garage where we keep all our spares. Just the way David likes it: spare toilet paper, spare baggies, backups of all our canned goods, and for me, of course, a generous backup supply of alcohol. I grabbed my favorite vodka and headed back inside. On the way in, I noticed a candy wrapper on the floor of the garage—a Dum Dum wrapper, to be exact—Mystery Flavor, if I was not mistaken.

I'll pick that up later, I thought to myself. My hands were a bit full. And right then, I had more important things to tend to.

Back in the kitchen, I pulled myself a nice long pour, then to the fridge for some juice. Damn it, again. I was out of cranberry juice. It would have to be Diet 7-Up today. I topped off my glass with a splash of the soda, and I headed back to the front of the house. I passed the mirror yet again. For the third time that day, I looked into the mirror, but this time I raised my glass, and looking into my own deep blue eyes, I mocked, "Here's looking at you, kid."

I regarded myself as I took a deep, long drink.

I HEARD THE GARAGE DOOR opening, announcing David's arrival, and I rushed to put things away before he came into the house. Had he come home early, or had I just lost track of time? He had Hannah in tow, and the two of them made a wonderful pair—his dashing, darker features and Hannah's fair, golden brilliance.

"Hello, my darlings!" I called out to them as they came through the door.

"Hi, Mommy!" Hannah yelled back as she came running into the kitchen.

"How was your day?" A generic question I know, but it's all I had right then. I received an "OK" from David and a "great" from Hannah. I immediately grabbed her and squeezed her tightly.

"I love you," I whispered into her golden hair.

"I love you too, Mama," she whispered back.

I had various items strewn across the kitchen, making

some sort of display that yes, dinner was underway. As I hurried over to give David a kiss, I noticed that he seemed a bit irritated. *Now what did I do? Or what didn't I do?* My mind raced through all the things I did that day, reviewing conversations and phone calls I had, errands I was supposed to have run. Did I miss something? What did I forget? But I came up with nothing. Oh well, we'll just ride this out and see what happens.

I finished the dinner preparations, and we all sat down to eat. Halfway through dinner and a lively conversation about Hannah's encounter with a badger on her field trip that day, David pulled out a Dum Dum wrapper and laid it carefully onto the dining room table. Hannah and I both fell silent. *Please, not now. Please, not now. Why now? Why this?* But he didn't hear my thoughts, and David started in.

"I found this in the garage," he quipped in a painfully torpid and measured manner. "Hannah, I believe we've had this conversation before, and this will be the last time. You are forbidden to eat Dum Dums from this point forward. And you," he turned his steely eyes to me, "are not to encourage this. She is to have no candy for the next two weeks."

Hannah immediately got tears in her eyes.

"I'm so sorry, Daddy. I must have missed that when I got out of the car. I'm so sorry."

Her anxiety level had just shot through the roof, our delightful dinner now ruined with this tirade. Why did he have to pick that precise moment to bring this up? She's eight, for Christ's sake. My heart ached for her and for myself. Why can't she just be a kid? David droned on about responsibility and taking care of things and blah, blah, blah. I was having a difficult time understanding how any of it related to a stray candy wrapper. I wanted to reach out to Hannah and hold her and tell her it's OK. She cried hysterically, and I was not doing much better. Maintaining on the outside, barely, but a complete wreck on the inside. I took a deep drink of my wine, wishing it was appropriate for eight-year-olds to drink so she could find the same solace. We finished our dinner in complete silence, Hannah and I choking down our food. Both of us had lost our appetite, yet to not finish our meal would be wasteful, and we don't want to be seen as ungrateful—not to mention the fact that neither of us wanted to supply David with any further ammunition.

LATER, AS I WAS DOING the dishes, I looked over at David while he poured over photo journals and his upcoming itinerary. I wondered what had happened to us. Everything was changing—me, our relationship. What started out as literally a fairy-tale romance had become—not an actual nightmare—but it had become so complacent, so ordinary, so regimented. Like the candy wrapper, like finishing my dinner even though, frankly, I didn't want to. Everyone always told me how lucky I was, how awesome David was, how handsome and rich, and how they would trade places with me in a heartbeat. They envied our lifestyle, my outward slender and attractive appearance, but if they knew what went on within the walls of this picture-perfect home, would they still feel the same way? We lived in a gorgeous home, Hannah went to one of the country's finest schools, we wanted for nothing, but at what cost? These questions continually appeared to pop in out of nowhere, and I found them most disturbing. I physically shook my head as if this motion would shake these inquiries out of my mind. I should be down on my fucking knees with gratitude for all David has done for us, yet at that moment, I felt anything but grateful.

What was wrong with me?

THE FIRST TIME I LAID EYES on David was electric. We met at a mutual friend's party. Well, for me, it was a friend of a friend of a friend. My age and lack of life experiences made me young and naive. David, older than me by a few years, had already established himself as quite the photojournalist. If you knew anything about any of that stuff, you would have recognized his name, but I sure didn't. It wasn't that he was famous or anything, just highly respected in his field. As I found out later, with digital photography, he had also heavily influenced the radical macrophotography technique and craze, one that made his photos stand out from the others. Notably distinctive, just like him.

My girlfriend Debra got word of this party from a friend of hers who had secured a position as a barmaid and got us onto the invitation list. Debra jumped at the chance to go, and I reluctantly agreed. Tired of the bar scene, I had simply resigned myself to the fact that true love had eluded me and would continue to do so until the day I died.

"To catch big fish, one must be shiny bait," Debra heartily laughed as she thrust forward a very low-cut, very tight, very sparkly dress. Debra was at least a full size smaller than me, and as she pulled the dress over my head and tugged it down over my hips and into place, I felt as though I might suffocate before we even left the apartment. Already a bit buzzed by the time we hit the party, I forgot about the constricting dress and found myself actually having a good time. The vibe the hosts created reminded me of a cross between Cirque du Soleil and the underworld. Men and women painted in lustrous silver from head to toe were serving cocktails and hors d'oeuvres on silver trays. The food and drinks were brightly colored, providing a vivacious contrast to the silver shimmering skin and trays. The entertainment included thong-wearing unicyclists, aerial ballet displays, and fire-breathing jugglers. There were firewalkers and acrobats balancing on poles no larger than the width of my thumb, all in gorgeous and suggestive costumes. I had never seen anything like it before. It was unnervingly unearthly.

This party generated a feast for the eyes and other senses, and it had an overtly hedonistic vibe to it. Enjoying all of it—the food, the drink, the disturbing beauty of the staff—it was the best time I'd had in a long while. Debra had disappeared, hooked up with some guy she saw on the way in, but I didn't mind. I was truly enjoying myself—until I wasn't. All of a sudden, I hit the wall, and a sense of panic overcame me. I didn't know any of these people. It seemed like things were getting weird and creepy in a most unwelcome way, and I was extremely drunk. I needed air. Between the thick crowd and the overpowering pulse of the music, I thought I might pass out. As I struggled to get to an exit, I locked eyes with a man. *I'm done for* dominated the thoughts flashing through my mind. I saw him reach out to me, and then everything went black.

When I came to, I found myself stretched out on a lounge chair on a balcony. The man I had locked eyes with sat next to me, grasping my hand while holding a cool cloth to my head.

When my eyelids fluttered open, he tipped up his cocktail and toasted, "Here's looking at you, kid."

And he took a swallow. I didn't know him. And it wasn't until later, much, much later that I discovered this chance encounter was anything but.

THINKING BACK TO THAT NIGHT always made me nostalgic for what could have been. Where did I go wrong; what wrongdoing made him stop loving me the way he had when we first met? And at that moment, like many moments before, I vowed to be a better wife, a better mother. They both deserved so much more than me. I was determined to measure up to his expectations. I slipped from around the counter, waving my dishcloth in the air. Going over to David on the couch, I eased myself carefully into his lap; I didn't want him to feel the extra weight I now carried. I slid the cloth behind his neck and pulled his mouth close to mine.

"Hey, mister photo man, you got any plans?" I used a low, breathy voice and finished it off with a deep kiss. He responded accordingly, and we retreated to our bedroom while Hannah remained behind, watching her favorite TV show.

After checking that box, it was time to put Hannah to bed. Even though I had put her to bed the night before, I wanted to again that evening. I started the shower for her, put in her favorite shampoo, and gathered up all her things.

"Baby, wash your hair first, please," I directed as she stepped under the stream of water.

"Mommmmm, why do I have to wash my hair?"

"Because it's dirty," I responded as gently as I could. She finished the shower with no further protests, and as I wrapped my little girl up in a fluffy oversized towel, I hugged her tightly while I patted her down and got her dry. On went the nightgown; we debated over underwear or no underwear. Oh gosh, I did not want her to grow up with the same hang-ups and shame about her body as I did, so no underwear it was.

She kissed her daddy good night, and then it was off to her room. We hadn't been in our new home for long, but we had made her room cozy and just perfect for our little girl. At eight, it couldn't be too babyish, and for a mom, it couldn't be too grown-up. It had just the right touches of magic and feminine appeal. That night, we read her favorite, *Frog and Toad*. Come to think of it, these were some of my favorite stories too, although I don't recall enjoying them as a child. She read a story, and then I read a story enjoying the antics of these two best friends. We continued to alternate a few times until she could no longer keep her eyelids open.

"Good night, my little angel. Sleep tight," I murmured against her neck. "I am the luckiest mommy ever to have you as my daughter."

"I'm lucky too, Mama," she replied. "You know, Daddy will never be satisfied."

David continued rifling through his stuff, so I headed back to our bedroom to read. In spite of the fact I was reeling from Hannah's parting comment, it didn't take long before my eyelids started to close, and I surrendered to sleep.

Another day. I had made it.

IT WAS SUNDAY MORNING, and I grabbed my coffee, and after a quick good morning to David, I headed up to my office. It was a dreary, overcast morning, and I flicked on all my lights to keep the gloom at bay.

It wasn't long before I heard, "Maggie, are you upstairs?"

"Yes,"

"That's a lot of lights on."

"Uh-huh," I mumbled as I read through my latest trade journal. A minute later, he came upstairs while turning off the lights. I looked up at him in disbelief; what the hell was he doing?

He started counting, "You have eleven lights on; why do you need eleven lights?" Why did he care how many bloody lights I had on?

I couldn't help myself. I knew it would only escalate things, but I attempted to explain the gloom outside and snapped back, "I have the lights on because I don't want to feel like I'm working in a dungeon."

"Yes, this is truly a dungeon, Maggie. Poor you, having to work in this absolute hellhole." There was no reasoning; there was no justifying. You'd have thought I'd have learned by now. My coffee had turned cold at this point, so I headed downstairs to refresh it and warmed it up with a little something special to calm my nerves.

THIS INTERACTION TOOK ME BACK to a night in the first year of our marriage when I still worked at the gallery. After several years of working in the gallery, I had been awarded the Curatorial Award for a particularly challenging artist. The man was brilliant, and David hated him. I was ecstatic about being assigned to the contract. I knew it would be demanding—the guy had a reputation, but I also knew that it would be an amazing opportunity. The minute I told David that I been granted the assignment, he warned me off the job. He ranted about the awful reputation this man had, how he took advantage of people and manipulated them, how I would be miserable working with him, and how I would never hold up under the working conditions. He continued with how the show would be a flop, as the guy was never satisfied, and how I would surely fail. Nothing David told me was anything I hadn't heard before, so I continued ahead with the project. As it turned out, Miles did challenge me, but not for the reasons I had been led to believe. We did not always agree on how the show should be presented, but his thoughtful intelligence in his reasons for wanting things a certain way made perfect sense. He would win no prize for Mr. Congeniality, but he never behaved in a demeaning or condescending manner.

One night at dinner, David seemed to be in a particularly good mood, so I began to share my insights about working with Miles.

"He's on his good behavior because he wants to sleep with you," David began.

"Oh no," I protested. "It's not like that at all; this is all about his work."

A wry smile crossed David's lips, "Is that so? You really are clueless; he would bed anything in a heartbeat, even you."

Something inside of me crumpled as he declared this. One minute I had been excited, happy, full of life force; I deflated in an instant, and every awful thing I'd ever thought about myself came flooding in. Tears sprung to my eyes, but

I didn't dare let David see. I got up from the table.

"Can I get you anything?" And I went to refill my glass.

THE INITIAL NOMINATIONS for the Curatorial Award came out, and I had been selected as one of the nominees. The jubilance was almost too much to bear. I couldn't remember ever feeling so happy, so hopeful, so proud of being recognized for something, anything. The night of the awards ceremony, David and I were both in our room getting ready. I wiggled into my new dress that I had scoured the city to find. I felt delicious in it. I brushed my hair and then attended to the final touches of my lipstick.

"Another new dress?" I recognized the tone, but I wanted that night to be perfect.

"Yes, don't you just love it?" I purred in my sexiest voice.

"Not bad, just think you could use the next size up."

Why now? Why did he have to do this right now, as I was preparing for the biggest night in my career?

"Oh, David," still with a smile plastered on my face, "Let's have fun tonight! I am so happy that I've been nominated, and I want to celebrate with you."

"Of course, you have. A monkey could win with Miles as the focus. Everyone fucking loves him," he snarled. I jerked back; he might as well have slapped me across the face. Suddenly, none of it mattered. I was a fraud. I did nothing to deserve this award; David was right. I stepped into the Uber, drink in hand, all alone. David had stormed off to god knows where, and without him to join me, I was tempted to stay at home rather than have to explain his conspicuous absence.

The elegant event pacified me a bit, although I was extremely self-conscious about being there alone. The champagne flowed when it was announced that I had won. A lump of anxiety remained in my stomach after the argument, leaving me with no appetite for food. Instead, I consumed the champagne, forcing myself back into a celebratory mood. That night, it didn't work. I felt guilty for celebrating, I felt undeserving, and I felt as though I was betraying David by coming without him. As soon as I could, I stole away, calling up a car on my phone. While waiting for my ride, I chastised myself for not grabbing one last flute of champagne before heading out the door.

I am an impostor in every sense of the word.

A failure as a wife, even though I couldn't fathom why David was so upset with me. An undeserving recipient of a prestigious award—I didn't even know who I was anymore. I heard a noise behind me and looked up. Miles was standing there with two drinks in his hand.

"Thank you," he complimented as he handed me a glass. I took it from him as he continued, "Pretty sure I'm not supposed to be out here with these, but I thought you could use one." I finished the champagne in two gulps. "Thank you and congratulations. You are a talented young lady..."

For some inexplicable reason, I couldn't even look at Miles, my head down, staring at the concrete spotted with discarded gum. I started to cry as he spoke, my ride pulling up to the curb. My head started shaking back and forth no, no, no—I pushed my glass back into his hands and fell into the car without a word.

The dark and cold house brought me no comfort when I returned. David was not there, and I thought how stupid I had been to rush home for nothing, what a fool I made of myself in front of Miles, and how I had let David ruin my entire evening. I made myself a quick drink, hung up my ridiculous new dress, and fell asleep.

DAVID CAME HOME and announced that our trip had been moved up because he'd been given an amazing opportunity to photograph the funeral proceedings of Nelson Mandela.

What? Wait. No, we can't take off even more time. Why do I always say no?

I sounded like a nagging, pissed off, spiteful wife. Why couldn't I just be happy and excited about this trip and whatever comes? Part of me brimmed with excitement. I'd never been on safari. I'd never been anywhere near that far away from home. This truly would be an adventure. Then reality set in. I knew why I could not be as happy and excited about it as I should be because all the preparation would be up to me. David surely wasn't going to help, and bless her heart, Hannah wanted to help in the worst way, but if something went wrong, it would be all my fault. My hands were tied. I would just have to work double-time in order to be able to get everything prepared for the trip. And so I began. There were clothes to be bought, special bags to acquire, appointments for shots (Hannah was not going to like that), airline tickets to be arranged for and purchased.

Thank goodness the contractor offered to handle all the lodging arrangements and transportation once we got there. But for the preparation, I was on my own. Papers to cancel, prescriptions to fill, mail to put on hold, notices to be sent, pet sitters to be hired, someone to water the plants. It felt as though the list would never end.

We were now going to be gone a full month, and it seemed as though I would never get it all done. I had consulted an arsenal of guidebooks and countless internet sites to make sure we were as prepared as one could possibly be and then some. It was a daunting task, but once I got into it, I took great pride in how much I had accomplished in such a short period of time. The mood at dinner that night felt light and, I daresay, festive. As we began talking about our trip and what we were looking forward to, Hannah told us a distressing story. She shared that a three-year-old went to Africa with her parents and got kidnapped from their campsite. The little girl was taken away, and she screamed and screamed. A lioness nearby heard the screams, mistaking the child's screams for that of one of her cubs. Running to retrieve her cub, she came upon the kidnappers and the young girl. The lioness rescued the child and kept her safe until her parents found her.

"Where in the world did you hear that story?" I

demanded, pissed that someone would put that awful scary thought in her head.

"I heard it at school."

"That's terrible," I said.

"I wouldn't mind."

"You wouldn't mind being kidnapped?"

"Not if I was kidnapped by lions." We each laughed at the absurdity of it all.

I guess it wasn't as scary to her as I thought it would be. I found myself doing that a lot—shielding her, protecting her, but protecting her from what? I couldn't be sure. The festive air had remained. The evening ended on a high note. I raised my glass in gratitude and poured myself another.

ON OUR WAY HOME from Girl Scouts, we stopped off at Chick-fil-A and grabbed some dinner to eat at home. We walked through the door, and Hannah tossed her backpack up onto the counter, kicked off her shoes, and dropped her coat onto the floor. She asked if she could watch TV. I raised my eyebrow and looked pointedly at the little pile she had just deposited.

"Oh, all right, Mom. Then can I watch TV?"

"Yes, then you can watch TV."

David came into the room and asked, "What's for dinner?"

"Well, you are in luck, kind sir, for we are having, wait for it—Chick-fil-A." I finished with a little laugh as I produced the bag that held our dinner.

"What, you didn't make anything tonight?"

"No, dear, we had Girl Scouts directly after school, and I spent most of the day preparing for our trip."

"And you had no time in there to prepare dinner?"

"But Daddy, I like Chick-fil-A," Hannah chimed in.

My heart seized every time Hannah had to witness these exchanges. I wondered what kind of an example I was setting while at the same time, I was thinking, "Oh, for fuck's sake. Is being the troop leader and all the other things I do not enough? I'm also expected to produce a proper dinner seven nights a week?"

It's times like these I wondered why we were still married.

THE FLIGHT OVER was not nearly as difficult as I had imagined. The upgraded seats were well worth the additional expense. Every inch counts when you are on an eighteen-hour flight. I passed the time reading and watching a couple of movies, but mostly I slept. A couple of Benadryl and wine with dinner ensured that I dozed off without too much trouble. Hannah stayed up all night watching movies, and David spent most of his time reviewing his work itinerary and shooting off emails to anyone he could think of.

I wondered if he knew how handsome he was? I pondered this as I looked over at him, deep in thought with his curly brown hair that always looked professionally mussed, his eyes the deep green color of emeralds from the mines of Zambia, the crooked lines of his nose that commanded attention but about which he never seemed self-conscious. I could never carry that off. I'd have it fixed on me in a heartbeat. I would also do something about the wrinkles that have invaded the area below my eyes, my hair that has been wispy since the day I was born and never seems to do anything, my boobs—too small. My thighs—too big. My butt—way too big. Yep, if it were up to me, I think I would scrap it all and start from scratch.

Sometimes I think I would have been better off as a man in the sense of not giving a damn about how I look, but such is life. The grass is always greener. Finally, without any resistance, the curtain came down over my eyes, and I thought of how lucky I was to be going to Africa and how even luckier that this captivating man had chosen me to be his wife.

SO FAR, the trip had gone smoothly and uneventfully, partly because of all my preparation and partly because the heavens were smiling down on me. We retrieved our rental car and loaded up our duffle bags. Although much warmer than home, there was no noticeable difference other than being surrounded by people with darker skin. At this point, we were trying to get out of the airport. We were all tired, feeling a little dirty, and somewhat out of our comfort zone in this great big country. We climbed into the car and set forth on our big adventure. After having to change sides in the car, for the steering wheel was on the right side of the car and we would be driving on the left-hand side of the road, I could already tell there was going to be trouble. David acted as though the placement of the steering wheel was a personal affront and intentionally placed there to make him look stupid. As we went around the roundabout to exit the airport grounds for the third time, he became convinced that somehow this was my fault.

"What kind of dumbshit, backward-ass people have the steering wheel on the right? Did you know about this, Maggie?"

Fascinating and scary, how his moods could swing back and forth so wildly. I considered myself a pretty laid-back kind of gal with not much that ruffles my feathers. It takes a lot in order for me to lose my cool. But with David, it is the complete opposite. I never could anticipate what was going to upset him or what would slide on by. Frequently, I felt as though I had been deposited in a field of shattered glass in my bare feet. I was hopelessly trapped in the center, and I could not escape without slicing myself into bloody ribbons.

WE FINALLY WAVED GOODBYE to the airport with a big cheer and headed toward our first destination, but we would not encounter the animals that we were so eager to see. That would have to wait. We would bide our time until the funeral of Nelson Mandela was over.

Once in the city, I began to notice some glaring differences. Johannesburg had previously been a thriving metropolis but no longer. I found myself witnessing poverty that

I had never seen the likes of—a poverty that was unimaginable and felt inhumane, although these were definitely humans—from the hijacked buildings, the garbage and sewage lining the street to the people, the broken people—men without limbs, children without clothes all lining the streets just like the trash. To some, they are one and the same, but to me, it was a devastating display of inhumanity. The conditions were beyond distressing, as poverty was not only in the city but spread across the country like a powerful disease. Makeshift homes in the way of tents and tin walls lined the highways and roads and stretched on for miles and miles on end, tarps for a roof if they were lucky. The living conditions here were deplorable. Many were consistently sick. Children played beside open sewage in their bare feet. Trash had been heaped up into piles and strewn about wherever one saw fit. The areas were riddled with violence so rampant and egregious that the police would not interfere or protect. There was no safety here; violence against women was particularly harsh. No fire department existed; the dwellings were made up of highly flammable materials that often resulted in a devastating loss of life and bodily harm caused by one careless act.

Townships they called them, but that can't be right; that almost made them sound livable. Yet, most of the people who lived in the townships were kindhearted, doing the best they could, showing courageous resiliency and creativity each and every day.

But there was no time to dwell on these injustices.

THE FUNERAL PREPARATIONS and proceedings went on for days. The country was in an official mourning period for ten days from his death. I knew Mandela had been a great man, but I knew little of him and the details and history of apartheid. Being in this country during that moment in history was eye-opening and heart-wrenching, to say the least. After witnessing the events over this ten-day span, I can only describe Nelson Mandela as a god on Earth. The more I learned about the history and the current conditions of this country, the dumber I felt. I vacillated between feeling hopeful for the future of my own country and hopeless in the knowledge that the atrocities mankind wages against each other are as old as the evolution of man. Africa is known as the cradle of mankind. Genocide, slavery, and unspeakable brutalities occurred between tribes and neighboring territories long before the first Dutch white man came onto the scene. And just like my own country, I realized there had been moments in time, moments in African history, when it was possible for whites and blacks to live and work together in harmony, in peace, and in love, yet due to ignorance, misunderstanding, and societal pressure, it never came to fruition. I also saw this issue to be far deeper than just black and white; it permeates every shade in between, and no one escapes this harsh reality. This wasn't a new thought, but the blatancy of it here in South Africa was shocking and began to change the way I understood the world.

I WAS GLUED TO THE TV in our hotel. David's schedule kept him busy going from one location to the next in order to cover all the happenings as they related to the mourning period for Nelson Mandela. I felt quite safe in our hotel and the staff, who were ninety-some percent black, couldn't have been kinder to Hannah and me. I had, however, been warned about venturing out alone, especially with a young child.

Hannah and I made the best of our time at the hotel.

We were certainly not roughing it. We quickly fell into a routine of sleeping in and enjoying a leisurely breakfast buffet down on the main floor. The foods were both unusual and familiar. Hannah was determined to try every flavor of juice; she began with the ones she knew: apple, orange, cranberry and then ventured out to try the less recognizable: pomegranate, baobab, hibiscus, tamarind, and many others. She and I both fell in love with the lilting, melodic way the employees all said "pleasure" when we thanked them. We loved it so much we started using it ourselves and laughed at each other with great delight.

I ordered my coffee with fresh milk and perused the buffet selections. I had never been a big breakfast eater, but the delectable feast in front of me was too tempting to turn away. I loaded my plate with banana, mango, and pawpaw, which is like a cross between these two—it quickly became my favorite fruit. Each morning there was an international cheese and meat selection unlike anything I'd seen before—a little Gruyère, karoo crumble, and I found a creamy mascarpone that was irresistible when paired with figs upon my wheat toast. Some mornings, I opted for cold cuts like pastrami or salami, and others I sampled the local hot dishes like savory chicken tikka, beef mince balls in chutney, or boerewors with sautéed mushrooms. I learned that centuries of European rule had left their mark on South African cuisine. In addition to her daily juice, Hannah typically went for a hot chocolate with extra whipped cream and whatever pastry looked good that day.

As we enjoyed our breakfast, my mind tended to wander. That morning, as I looked at my divine daughter, a million thoughts came rushing in. She is so kind, so smart, and so emotionally in tune, this young girl. As I watched her interact with the world and the people within it, I was touched by how compassionate and thoughtful she is. She was so respectful and engaging of the people around her, whether it's a peer, a person of authority, and especially now, the personnel catering to our every need here in our little hotel bubble. Between the culture, the language, and the accents, there were challenges in communication. Hannah had a smile for everyone, and they, in turn, lit up when she spoke to them. Her demeanor truly reflected that a stranger was just someone she hadn't met yet, and everyone we encountered responded in kind. I couldn't help but be so proud of her. I thought back to all the moms I knew who insisted they could never travel that far away with their kids, which made me sad for them because I didn't think I could ever travel that far away without her. She was such a wonderful travel companion.

Getting to experience the world through her eyes was a true gift.

MY PREGNANCY WITH HANNAH was not an easy one. I wasn't sick or anything, hardly at all, actually. The circumstances of my pregnancy were extremely emotionally taxing. Because David and I had waited to have children, mine was considered a geriatric pregnancy—as if! There were complications with the umbilical cord, and they were convinced the baby was going to have Down syndrome. The only other person who knew this was David. When they asked us if we wanted to have an amniocentesis done to determine for sure, it didn't take us any time at all to decline once we heard there was a risk of having a miscarriage due to the procedure. This baby would be ours no matter what. The possibility added a lot of strain. I didn't share it with anyone, not because I was ashamed or hiding it. Rather, I didn't want the added worry or pity energy out in the world. I had been scared of what that might mean for us, for me. Just like the preparation for this trip, I knew the vast majority of the caretaking, the researching, finding the right support for our baby, would fall on my shoulders. I knew that having a child would alter our lives dramatically, especially mine. But having a child with special needs would completely put an end to life as I knew it. This thought was suffocating and bleak, and I remember feeling ashamed for being so selfish and self-centered. I prayed diligently and lit a candle on the Notre Dame campus grotto in hopes of having a "normal" child.

The day of her delivery arrived. Due to the concerns and complications, and because our baby was in a breech position, I had been scheduled for a C-section. I lost count, but the delivery room swarmed with a hospital team anticipating what might happen with the birth.

I was convinced I was having a boy, but when the doctor announced, "Maggie, your daughter just peed on me," an overwhelming sense of relief and boundless joy swept through my body.

I never understood the meaning of the word swoon until Hannah was born. I mean, I understood the definition, but it was an emotion or feeling that I had never experienced for myself, and when I came across it in literature, I found it applied to silly women. But when Hannah arrived, it was another story. I had waited so long for this child that when my doctor announced she was a girl, I swooned for the first time in my life. If I had been upright instead of stretched out and cut open on the operating room table, I would have fallen off my feet. The combination of sheer ecstasy, joy, and boundless love took over and flooded every cell of my body. I haven't been able to recapture that emotion, but I can remember it, which will have to suit me for the rest of my life.

I LOOK AT HER NOW, and call me crazy, but ever since the moment her arrival was announced, I knew she was a chosen one. This remarkable child would touch the lives of many from that day forward. I tried not to say it out loud too often, but I called her my golden child. Her glossy hair that looked like spun gold, her pale skin, her sunny disposition, her bright future, it all went together.

I had visions of Hannah before she was born. I could never see her face; she was always standing beside me or in front of me. One time, I dreamt we were standing in a field, and she was far, far ahead of me. As the memory of this dream came back to me, I saw the details of the field. The golden grass came up about waist-high on me. As Hannah walked forward, the grasses parted to make way for her to pass through. She headed somewhere specific, but I did not understand the significance of this. I knew I should accompany her, I desperately wanted to accompany her, but I was frozen to the spot where I remained. All I could make out was a dark silhouette of her little body as it moved further and further away. I could see her, but she was so far away. I called to her to the point where my voice became hoarse, but she never turned around, never slowed her gait. She just kept moving through the field, singing all the way. Remembering this dream left me disappointed in myself. It was clear that I knew I was going to have a girl all along, yet I was so untrusting of myself, of what I knew to be true, that not only did I not listen to my inner knowing, but I completely contradicted myself. This is what my life had become, ignoring everything I knew to be true about myself and letting everyone and everything influence and dictate my decisions. I tried to remember the last time I had been deeply, truly happy and came up short.

HANNAH AND I TOOK our time finishing our breakfast; we were typically one of the last tables to leave the restaurant and head back to our room. I flipped on the TV to see the morning broadcast. This was the day that nearly one hundred heads of state, representatives, royalty, and as reported, ninety thousand mourners headed out to attend the official memorial. The memorial took place in the FNB Stadium in Johannesburg. I found it curious that only ninety "important" people were reported to be in attendance. For a stadium that holds nearly one hundred thousand people, I would have expected so many more. It seemed to me that a man who was hailed as a hero by so many throughout the world, whose good deeds and actions impacted more than forty million people in South Africa and heavily influenced civil rights movements around the globe, would have garnered the attention and respect of more than ninety world leaders and dignitaries. It made me question if only lip service was being paid to his great works. It also made me wonder how many prominent people would have come to his memorial if he had been white.

The rain descended upon Johannesburg; the quintessential angels were weeping over the death of this beloved man. I looked out the window of our hotel room, and along with the rain, I noticed the trees were weeping too. Each individual leaf had a large drop of water upon it. I was certain that if I were close enough, I would be able to see my reflection in each droplet, and I wondered what that reflection would show me. The leaves quivered as each drop of water from the clouds above hit and, in turn, fell to the ground. There was a silver curtain of rain behind the trees, beating down at a steady pace with no sign of letting up. A few stray drops splashed upon the window. Even above the noise of the television, I could hear the repeated tap as drops struck the window and then, ever so slowly, dribbled down the glass. When I turned back to the TV, I noticed I had a drink in my hand and tears were dripping down the side of my face.

The rainy weather added to the solemnness and gravity of the occasion. I could see the sheets of rain coming down through the lens of the TV camera, and I heard mournful, yet spirited, singing coming through the loudspeakers of the stadium. Not everyone wore black. As the cameras panned through the crowd, the mourners of South Africa were wearing all the colors of the flag: green, red, yellow, white, and black and T-shirts emblazoned with pictures of Tata: so many called him "Father." The close relatives and dignitaries were all dressed in black and had somber expressions to match. But the people, his people, were there to celebrate this man. The rain did not dampen their spirit; they were singing along, they were jubilant, and I marveled at the resiliency of the wondrous people of this awe-inspiring country. Flags and banners with Mandela's beaming face upon them were sprinkled throughout the stadium.

When the current president, Jacob Zuma, waved to the

crowd as he arrived to take his seat, he received a hostile reception. The crowd erupted into boos and jeers over the unyielding poverty, crime, and lack of jobs. And just as quickly, the mourners were soon singing and chanting, reminding me of a soccer match I once attended. Being an open-air stadium, the people were protecting themselves from the elements with rain gear, trash bags, tarps, and umbrellas. I watched intently, enraptured with the scene unfolding before me, and wondered if I would catch a glimpse of David. It was probably a bit of morbid curiosity, but I also wondered what was in store for this country, what was ahead for these people who had desperately loved this influential man. I watched these proceedings with rapt interest, mourning the death and celebrating the life of the man who had brought me here.

As I had these thoughts, an eerie stillness and quiet overcame our hotel room. I couldn't seem to put words to it, but it felt as though all the air had been sucked out of the room, and I found it difficult to breathe, my heart pounding wildly. My mind flashed to Hannah, and I immediately called to her in the other room.

"Yes, Mommy?" she replied.

"Oh nothing, just making sure you're OK," I faltered.

"I'm OK. Are you OK?"

"Yep, I'm fine, sweetheart." Undeniably, I was anything but.

The memorial continued to unfold on the screen before me. The entire affair lasted nearly four hours.

David didn't return to our hotel until long after Hannah and I had finished dinner. We snuggled on the couch in the sitting area, watching a movie she had brought along with us. As he burst through the door, I could tell he was in a snit. Well, who wouldn't be after standing out in the heavy rains all day?

The feeling of despair washed over me as David lashed out, "What is SHE still doing up?"

Completely taken aback, I said, "David, Hannah is still up because we were enjoying a movie while we were waiting for you."

"She should be in bed and asleep by now."

"Sweetheart, we are on vacation—yes?"

I glanced over, and my heart broke as Hannah sat frozen on the couch with tears streaming down her sweet little cheeks. Belle and the Beast were mid-waltz, suspended in time on the TV while David continued his rant.

"How marvelous for the two of you to be on vacation while I am out there working my ass off. Must be nice."

I took a deep breath. "OK, Hannah, honey, let's take a nice soothing shower, and Mommy will tuck you in. We will pick up with Belle and the Beast tomorrow."

"It's OK, Mama, I understand. I just wish he didn't yell so much," my angel whispered to me.

"David, darling, why don't you grab yourself something to drink and relax while I get Hannah to bed?"

"I don't need to relax; I need to sleep. Keep it down. And turn that shit off."

Yes, David, darling, I will turn that shit off. I will turn it all off, so I don't have to witness the devastation while you tear us all apart and leave nothing but splinters in your wake.

THE STATE OF OUR CURRENT relationship bore no resemblance to when we first began dating. Our first night together made me believe in love, made me believe I had found my soul mate at long last. The evening of David's show had finally arrived, and it was a terrific success. As always, there was plenty of champagne. The buyers were free with their wallets, and the critics were free with their praise. I watched David from afar as he worked the room. When he turned it on, he turned it on like no one else. Everyone clamored for his attention. He hadn't mentioned it earlier, so I was a bit surprised when near the end of the evening he asked me to come home with him for the night.

I was nearly breathless when I responded, "Yes, I'd love to."

This would be our first time together, and I felt slightly sick to my stomach with nervousness and excitement, and oh my god! Just before midnight, he grabbed my hand and told me it was time to go. He extracted a bottle of champagne and two glasses, and we headed to the door but not before we ran into a colleague of David's who winked at me lasciviously and related something to David out of earshot. Somehow, between all that was going on, David had ordered a driver to take us back to his apartment. He popped the champagne, and we toasted to such a terrific show and a triumphant evening.

He looked deep into my eyes and toasted one more time. "To new beginnings. Here's looking at you, kid."

His mouth moved over mine, and he kissed me so deeply and with such urgency that I could feel my toes begin to tingle. I felt a bit embarrassed with the driver right there, but fortunately, we soon arrived at David's place. He took my hand as I left the car, and since it had begun to drizzle, we trotted to the front entrance of his building. In the elevator, he grabbed my face using his hands and, with a full-frontal press, pushed me up against the wall of the lift. I couldn't help myself; I had waited for this for so long. Moans that generated from the base of my throat began to escape my mouth, and I shuddered with the anticipation and the deliciousness of it all. Here was the fairy tale coming true in this precise moment. I took my right leg and hiked it up over his left hip and waist, so glad I wore ridiculously high heels tonight. At this moment, they were certainly an advantage. I pressed back against him with the same fiery urgency that he expressed with his hands, his tongue. I would simply die if this man did not completely consume me at this moment. My pussy throbbed and pulsed to its own beat. We tumbled out on his floor. Both of us found it difficult to make forward progress, so hungry were we for each other. David was juggling his keys, trying to get the right one that would unlock the door to our newfound paradise. Once inside the door, David wheeled me around and pressed me up against the back of the entry door, just as in the elevator, so we could pick up where we left off. Only this time, our clothes started dropping to the floor. My entire insides started to itch; I needed to feel him inside of me.

Oh David, what are you doing to me? It is so exquisite.

The last article of clothing to go were my panties that David removed as he knelt to the floor and lowered his mouth onto my exposed vulva. I withered in complete ecstasy and cried out as he tasted me. We made it to his bed, and I finally received the relief my body had been screaming for as he slowly, teasingly, positioned himself inside of me. I clawed at his back, and the moans became more primal and guttural, his face buried in my hair as he whispered my name over and over again. I had waited so long for someone to love me like this. As the fire was extinguished with one final thrust, we collapsed beside each other, trying to catch our breath.

David's head was still buried in my hair, and he murmured, "Maggie, don't ever leave me."

"I wouldn't dream of it," I whispered so quietly I'm not even sure he heard me.

WE HEADED INTO the national park. Hannah and I were so excited, and David seemed to be as well. We were barely through the park gates when we saw our first African animal—an impala. He was a young one and so sweet. Standing next to the side of the road, his fur the color of toffee shined in the sunlight. We were close enough that I could see the bug bites where his fur slightly raised in places all over his body. His ears were alert, but he seemed quite relaxed with the cars passing by. His hindquarters were a cotton ball white, marked with an unmistakable "M" on his rump. We were to find out later, the impalas are known as the McDonald's of the plains, both for the conspicuous "M" and the fact that practically every other animal uses them as a source for food. Pretty funny unless you're an impala. As we continued on, we saw animal after animal after animal unlike any I had ever seen: giraffes, baboons, monkeys, elephants, a cheetah, zebras, water buffaloes, rhinoceroses.

We came to a watering hole, and it was like a scene from the *Lion King*. The first thing that jumped out at me were the four Cape buffalo standing knee-deep in the water, sipping from it below. All four of them had their muzzles in the water while their eyes drifted upward, always on alert. The horns atop their heads looked like massive helmets as though they were perpetually ready for battle, and I supposed that, indeed, they were. A great white egret coming in for a landing had yet to touch the water. Its wings fanned out, its legs stretched long, hovering over the water. For just a split-second, the reflection in the still water created a magical effect before she lightly touched down. On the opposite side of the watering hole waded a pod of eight hippos; most of them appeared to be young, with one massive hippo leading the charge. It took a while to figure out that two of them were submerged in the water with only a slight portion of their back visible above the surface. They looked like rocks from where we were stationed on the road.

On the banks of the water were all kinds of animals, all grouped together as if being forced to segregate. The turtles were sunning themselves on a log by the side of the water. Baby monkeys were climbing all over their mothers trying to suckle at sagging teats while Mama Monkey attempted to walk. I laughed at this scene because I could so relate. There are days I can't even have a moment in the bathroom to myself before Hannah comes barging in or the dog pushes the door open with her nose. I was curious if the Mama Monkey felt as trapped and resentful as I did at times.

I loved being a mother; I had envisioned having kids my whole life. But what no one told me were all the expectations of all the roles to fulfill that I would succumb to. Of course, I wanted to be the perfect mother, the perfect wife. As with most things, I took it to the extreme of perfectionism in order to prove my worth. I made my own baby food, we tried cloth diapers for a spell, and when I couldn't keep up and switched to disposable, I felt like a failure. I stopped breastfeeding because David insisted it was cutting into our social life. Our social life? More like his social life when I refused to breastfeed in public. I still hadn't forgiven myself for that.

Due to my perfectionistic tendencies and my self-imposed impossible expectations, I had set myself up for being a failure as a mother. Hannah was an extraordinary little girl, and I loved her beyond anything I knew I was capable of. I, alone, had created the circumstances that most times, when I looked at her, I saw all the ways I was lacking as a mom. By making myself available 24/7, yes, there were times I felt resentful for not keeping part of me just for myself.

The zebras clumped together at the water's edge, lapping from the surface of the water. The birds, I didn't know what the birds were, but they were magnificent. There were little brown birds with bright yellow beaks. The sparse vegetation left few trees for shade and not many hiding places for predator or prey. This was truly the most magnificent sight I had ever beheld, and it made tears fall from my eyes, but we had to move on if we were to make it to camp before nightfall, which we must because they would lock the gates and not reopen until morning. I was deeply disappointed that we had to move on so quickly. I wanted to linger in this moment. I wanted to savor it.

I wanted to memorize it for the rest of my life.

WE ARRIVED AT CAMP literally with only
minutes to spare. Our accommodations were breathtaking.
The bungalow as a whole was mostly neutral in nature. A
rather inviting bed immediately captured my eye. Mosquito
netting suspended above the bed on some kind of bamboo
frame draped elegantly and was pulled to the side with
ties to allow entrance to the bed. Crisp white linens with a
tailored bed skirt completed the look. The effect created a
sense of simplicity. The floor was deep mahogany in color,
almost identical in color to Amos, who had carried our
bags and shown us to our bungalow. Knotted wool rugs
and animal hides were generously dispersed about. The
walls were a creamy and attractive shade of beige. Various
antlers and artwork were sprinkled throughout the rooms.
A little wood desk similar to one we had at home in our
kitchen called you to sit for a moment and dash off a letter
to a loved one. I admired the remaining furniture, a mix of
leather, wicker, and natural fibers. The only color provided
came from the patterns in the rugs, a festive throw pillow,
or a splash of bright pigment in a painting. I was ready to
move in. Hannah grabbed Dolly, jumped onto the bed,

whipped off the ties that were holding the netting in place, and immediately closed herself in a self-imposed hideout. I laughed and filled with pleasure at her enthusiasm and imagination. She never ceased to amaze me. Her pure joy as she takes in the world around her, her resiliency when she encounters something harsh, and her compassion for humans and animals alike was inspiring. I knocked on the "door" of the bed and asked to come in. I could use a little escape. She welcomed me with great flourish and beckoned me inside.

"Thank you, my lady," I chirped in some made-up British accent.

She giggled back with, "Pleasure."

We burst into laughter; I grabbed her around the waist and pulled us both down onto the mattress. We lay there staring up at the rich beam-covered ceiling of this entrancing room, and she rolled over half on top of me and whispered, "Do you think we will see any lions, Mama?"

"Ohhh, I don't know what we are going to see, but if it's lions you want to see, I bet we do. Haven't you heard? All the guides have been going around for weeks telling the lions that little Hannah is coming to Africa and wants to see them!"

"Oh, Mom, really!" and we started laughing again.

She placed one hand onto my arm and ran her other hand through my hair, "Don't be scared, Mama. Everything is going to be OK."

I was taken aback for just a moment; it's like this child could see right through me to the depths of my soul.

I kissed her on the forehead, and as I reached out to tickle her, in a lighthearted voice, I replied, "Yes, my dear, everything IS going to be OK unless I get eaten by one of those lions!"

I slipped from the bed, and as I began to unpack, Hannah began to sing of the lions she was about to meet.

We had missed dinner, but our hosts were so gracious that after welcoming us and allowing us some moments to get settled in our quarters, they brought us to the dining area, and we were served a kindhearted and generous meal with no one rushing us. I was too tired and too mystified to even ask what it was that we were eating. I think part of me just didn't want to know. Whatever they were serving, it was delicious. Even Hannah, whom I'd indulged in being a picky eater, ate her meal in silence and without question. I wondered if she had been captivated by these animals and this country the way I had. I thought she had, at least to some extent. She had always loved animals and wanted to be near them.

My magical Hannah. I envied her curiosity about the world and the way she could walk into a room and make an impact on ninety percent of the people by the time she left. I'm certain she got this engaging quality from David, but if I were to compare the two, his impact demanded respect, where her pure light of joy invited all to shine.

As I could have predicted, the staff—all of the black men and women—fell in love with her immediately. Many of them knew just a little English, and most of the communication was spoken in their own tribal and mixed languages: Zulu, Xhosa, and Afrikaans being the most common. They were genuinely considerate of us, and the food and the wine were flowing. I felt myself melting into the experience, and I slipped my hand into David's. He squeezed it gently and held it for a few moments before releasing it and digging back into a second plate of whatever it is that they were serving. It had been a big day for us—a big sensational, magical day unlike anything I could have imagined in my wildest dreams.

Maybe this trip won't be so bad after all.

WE ONCE HOSTED a dinner for a group of under-lings that David had mentored. I knew he needed it to be just perfect and to portray a certain image. I love planning parties, but with his constant interruptions, injections, and criticisms, I could not wait for this event to be over. Finally, the evening of our dinner arrived. His students filed in with their dates, and David could not have been more charming. As I watched from the doorway, I envied the attention he lavished onto his guests. He was so charming and courteous of the men and women alike, complimenting them in areas where they thought they were flawed, telling outrageous and outlandish stories, causing uproarious laughter. He made sure all wineglasses were full and made each and every person there feel invited, important, and wanted—just as he had made me feel when I first met him. The ultimate Prince Charming; I could see the glow of admiration and appreci-ation on the faces of each and every guest. He had told me about one of his students, a rather homely girl whom he thought quite dim and didn't belong in the program but who was only there because of her familial relations with someone at the photography school. Laying in bed one night, I distinctly remember him telling me what a "stupid little bitch" she was.

I noticed him speaking with her in a corner of the room. He had his back to me, but I could clearly see Marianne's face. Her eyes were shining from a tad too much wine; I recognized the look. Her head thrown back, she laughed rather lustily at some joke David had just told her.

As I walked past to the dining room, I saw him lift his arm to clink glasses and overheard him say, "Here's looking at you, kid."

Before I even knew what happened, the glass fell from my hand and ruptured on the floor, splashing wine all over my legs and David's new linen pants. I stumbled a bit but caught myself before I fell to the ground as well. David's eyes flashed with venomous rage, but his voice betrayed nothing as he grabbed my arm and queried, "Oh Maggie, are you all right? Are you not feeling well?"

I felt fine, just self-conscious in the face of humiliation. Joselyn, one of the staff assisting us that night, came and helped me clean up the mess. When the night came to an end and it was time for all to head home, we gathered near the entryway and offered our goodnights. Everyone raved about what a wonderful evening it was, and more than one person told me what a gem David was and how lucky I was.

I found it hard to be gracious but did my best to smile and say thank you.

I wasn't feeling very lucky.

WE WOKE BEFORE DAWN, eager to join the other guests in the main rondoval. We were not allowed to walk in camp unescorted when it was dark. We were ready to go before Amos arrived to collect us. David muttered about this stupid escort rule, so when Amos finally appeared at our door, I was elated. Amos was the blackest, largest man I had ever seen. I couldn't honestly even see him in the dark. All I saw were two friendly, laughing eyes and the biggest, widest smile there on our front porch. We moved briskly to the rondoval in order to grab some coffee and a biscuit prior to getting on the road before sunrise. We would be served a proper breakfast upon our return. We climbed onto the truck. Because Hannah was so small and so young, she had been positioned up front between the driver and our guide. David and I slid into the seats behind her. Although it was coming into summertime there, we huddled together under blankets provided to us by our hosts to eradicate the morning chill, and off we went. If I thought our drive into the park the day before was magical, this was exceptional. When I knew we were going on safari, I had the impression that we would be sitting in a truck somewhere, passing binoculars around, watching some horizon, waiting for an animal to show up. So wrong. The guides and drivers from all the different camps worked together in order to give their guests the best experience possible. We drove along and then turned at what seemed to be the most improbable spot and pulled up within feet of the animals, no binoculars necessary.

I'm ashamed to admit it, but my experience and familiarity with African animals consisted of only what I'd seen in the movies and at our zoo. The hyenas quickly became one of my favorites to watch. The posture of their front shoulders hunched over the top with their heads hanging down and the back of their spines sloping downward to sinewy legs insinuate wickedness for sure. Yet, their little faces are so sweet and adorable. These small creatures are the epitome of resilience. No one respects them, they are last to the party, left nothing but scraps, but in spite of all that, they thrive. The elephants are defyingly enormous. I referred to them as ghosts because when they walked behind our truck, they did not make a sound. If it weren't for the crackling of the branches breaking in their wake, you would never know they were there. The only thing not enchanting was the persistent and pervasive mist. It coated everything like a blanket and added to the chill in the air. We were told it was most unusual for that time of year. It was like something straight out of a horror movie, and I couldn't shake the feeling of foreboding.

There were so many different animals to see. It appeared as if they were prostrating themselves to us in the most magnificent way, as if to say, "I am here. See me. Know me."

That first day, before heading back to camp, we heard a noise that sounded at first like a low rumble. Sitting so close to our guide and driver, I could tell something big was happening.

The way Christiaan was chattering away on his radio in a language I did not understand and the quick sudden movement and changes in the direction of our vehicle, I wondered what it could be. The vehicle moved rapidly through the bush, and as we got closer, it became obvious what we had heard. It was a lion, a giant male lion roaring, calling to his pride, our guide explained as we got within sight of this magical beast.

Christiaan started to say that this lion is the head of the Maasakai Coalition, when Hannah yelled out, "It's Numbalo!"

"Yes," Christiaan acknowledged, "that is Numbalo, but we have not seen him for months." When Numbalo rose from the grass and began to move, we followed him from a safe distance. "See how he is favoring his left leg? He has been badly injured. He will soon be displaced from his position with the Maasakai."

Hannah spoke up again, "I know. We are here to say goodbye."

Everyone in the truck tittered a little at the precocious young girl naming a lion and commented, "What a sweet thing that was to say; what a darling little girl."

But I knew differently. Hannah had been saying things like this for about the past three years. She could know things without the ability to know things. I was dumbfounded that she had known the name of the lion before ever hearing it, for it turned out Numbalo was, in fact, his name. Yes, she was a highly empathetic little girl, but it went way beyond that. She was keenly attuned to the feelings, emotions, and moods of other people. Lately, when she met someone, she could literally "read" their life and walk away knowing that person's circumstances and what they were experiencing internally just by engaging with them for a few moments. These interactions often affected her physically, either leaving her exhausted and grumpy or energized and joyful, depending on the person. I didn't understand it completely myself; being intuitive was the closest description I could land on. But I had never seen her do this where animals were involved, and it struck me we were brought to Africa for a reason and each one of us would leave a profoundly different person. This realization only increased my levels of anxiety and unease.

EACH RIDE BROUGHT MORE and more delights in the way of getting to observe and meet new animals. To see them in their natural habitat stirred a longing deep inside of me. It felt like I was the one in a cage and the animals had come to view me. What a weird thing to think, I pondered, but the uneasiness of being in a cage would not leave me.

Where do I come up with these things?

As we continued along one afternoon, we came across a dead rhinoceros. Christiaan tried to skirt around it, but it was too late. We were all but on top of it. And by dead, I mean the poor creature had been slaughtered. We had heard stories about poaching, but never could we have envisioned in our bloodiest thoughts how awful and devastating it truly is. The animal had been slaughtered in one of the most inhumane ways—all for its horns. This type of senseless, wasteful killing has been going on since the 1200s when the first traders inhabited Africa. The Chinese wanted the horns because they believed it would make them virile, helping them get and maintain erections. It is astonishing that people believed these horns had magical powers still today, and this was what they left behind. They did not take the meat that could sustain an entire village for a month, but rather, they stripped the horns with a saw from the rhino's regal face and left the animal there to bleed to death. The traps they use are horrendous, and they do nothing to help put the animal out of its misery.

What a sickening waste.

ONE AFTERNOON, before we left camp, Christiaan asked Hannah what animals she would like to see that day as if ordering off a menu. She declared she still wanted to see a cheetah, a wild dog, and a secretary bird. I laughed, for I learned that in the land of animal viewing, she might as well have asked to see flying pigs and thrown in a unicorn for grins. Within the space of two hours, Christiaan had managed to find all but the wild dog.

"Don't worry, sweet Hannah," he cajoled. "I have something extraordinary to show you and your family if you'll let them come along," and he winked.

He drove along the path and turned into a dry riverbed. Pulling the truck into the brush at an angle, he snapped off the engine and explained, "Now we wait!"

It couldn't have been more than a few minutes of silence when out of the brush tumbled three *adorable* lion cubs. I can't even express in words the wonder and preciousness at the sight of them. They leaped over and under each other in the most outrageous of displays as if they were putting on a comedy show. They had us all laughing and enjoying ourselves, particularly Hannah. Several moments passed by before we heard a thunderous roar; Numbalo sprang from the bushes and practically landed inside our truck while the cubs scattered in every direction. Hannah regained her composure and told us that Numbalo was furious with his children for coming out to play.

She leaned back between my legs and whispered, "He needs help."

I agreed with her; he did need help. Numbalo's

condition had worsened, and the extent of his injuries was grave. I didn't understand that wasn't the help she meant he needed, and I tried my best to comfort Hannah.

THE NEXT SEVERAL DAYS came and went with continuing mysteries of Africa revealing themselves to us. Hannah became the best of friends with the head cook's daughter, Behatti. Although Behatti was even younger than Hannah, that made no difference in Hannah's mind, nor did the color of her skin. Growing up in Africa and spending the majority of her young life on the reserve had made Behatti super smart. She knew almost as much about the animals as the guides did, and she and Hannah were kindred souls. In between rides, the girls would look for each other and find a place to play. Behatti knew a little English, but language was no barrier for these two girls; they were truly like peas in a pod.

Akilah tried to discourage the relationship at first, feeling that a daughter of the staff should not impose herself upon the guests. But the friendship had been formed, and when she saw my delight for Hannah to have such wonderful company, Akilah stopped objecting. I was happy that Hannah had someone young to play with. She had been around adults her whole life. All my friends had kids who were much older and certainly not into play dates with our eight-year-old.

Come to think of it, I no longer had any close girl-friends. When David and I started dating, it became clear that our childish antics and pastimes weren't of any interest to him. Dive bars and cheap activities were beneath him. It was easier then to just go along with the pleasures that David was into. After all, I found lectures, film screenings, photography shows, and black-tie events to be exciting as well. I guess after saying "no thanks" enough times, the invitations from my friends stopped coming. David certainly didn't think very highly of the company I was keeping, so the dissipation of friends in my life didn't bother him one bit. In fact, I think it rather pleased him.

Hannah and Behatti forged a friendship within days that was worthy of my envy.

My whole life, I had craved female friendships. I noticed they had always been there for my taking and enjoyment, but I had shut myself away from them. I had closed them off by neglecting, sabotaging, or holding out because I had no confidence that a woman who truly got to know me could hold all the parts of me. If she ever found out who I truly was, she would no longer like me, much less love me.

I was so lonely.

Typically, they played on the front porch of our quarters or in the gardens beside it, as I would read or rest or join them on the porch. I would feel such a joy as the giggles floated on the wind or as a burst of laughter cut through the air like a knife. Behatti was not allowed to join us on any of the rides, but Hannah would return and share every detail of our adventures with her.

Even if she couldn't understand all that Hannah was saying, Behatti would respond with legends and stories that she had been told by her grandmother, aunts, and uncles in broken English as best she could. It was truly a pity that we would be leaving here in a short time; these girls could learn so much from each other.

MY FAVORITE PART of the rides was the sundowners. The custom in the late afternoon was the truck would pull over as the sun was just beginning to set and we would have a happy hour—but the most unusual happy hour I had ever had. It was more like tailgating. A makeshift table would pop out of the back of the truck and a bar right along with it.

They would prepare for us our drink of choice, and for now, mine was a gin and tonic. They had little bowls filled with potato chips and biltong, an air-dried, marinated beef snack. Oh, nothing could taste as delicious as this. We were always near a body of water so we could see the animals come down for their evening drink as the heat of the day began to dissolve and night came on. If you've ever seen an African sky at sunset, then you know what I mean when I say it is truly God's country. The sky turns thousands of different shades of color, starting from barely pink to an orange and red that is so vivid you would swear the sky was on fire. The trees are silhouetted in pitch black, as are any of the remaining animals and birds that fly through the scene unfailingly.

EVERY NIGHT SINCE we came across Numbalo, we could hear his roar, often during our sundowners, a roar so powerful that it shook in your chest and made you want to be a part of whatever is out there, a roar so strong and mighty that I was halfway convinced our guide was wrong when it came to the fact that this wondrous beast was dying. Hannah commented more than once about this creature's impending death.

She told me, "He is calling for his tribe to remain strong. He is getting weaker and weaker by the day, and he is worried that if his tribe doesn't stay together, the entire Maasakai Kingdom will be destroyed."

I knew in my heart she was right. Christiaan heard this as well and didn't disagree. Spending the hours beside this little girl, he had come to know that there was something special about her, and I was so grateful that he did not disparage, contradict, or condescend to her when he spoke to her. When he listened, he listened carefully and encouragingly while she spoke.

As I had heard this tale now a few times from her, I found it curious that she hadn't shared her story with her dad. It's not my place to do so, but I knew he'd be angry if he found out I was keeping it from him.

The drinks, the scenery, the ambiance, the roaring all contributed to this being my favorite part of the day, a tradition I felt I must continue at home. It is on this thirteenth night that we caught sight of the animal we had been hoping to see for quite some time. On our way back to camp, after the sundowner, we spotted—or I should say our guide tracked—a leopard up in a tree. She had company. Near this stunning creature lay a much smaller leopard, her cub, and an impala that she had slain for her family. With her powerful jaws, she had dragged the animal up into the high branches of the bushwillow tree. The guide and drivers shined their spotlights up into the tree for us all to see the mama, her baby, and her kill.

It was unlike anything I'd ever witnessed. I did wonder how I would react to something like this when we were home preparing for our trip. I found it so curious that I felt badly for the impala, but for a moment, I was primarily over-come with awe and wonder—the wonder of how a leopard, not much larger than the impala, could have the strength to kill it, much less the fortitude to haul it straight up a tree.

I marveled at just how intricate and necessary and inter-twined we all are, how none of us get out of this alive, how dependent we are on one another even if we don't want to be, and all the magical things that happen in between. It made me weep. It was all so moving. When we returned to camp, a celebration was in the air. Although many different people had come and gone from the camp during the time that we were there, no one had seen a leopard until tonight, and that certainly called for a celebration.

Earlier in the day, Christiaan had told us a story about the Marula tree and the fruit it bears. I decided that would be my drink of choice on this fine evening. The dinner was scrumptious. I had stopped asking what we were having; I simply ate it. Although I could be amazed by the circle of life, I preferred to be a bit ignorant when it came to my part in it.

I AWAKENED FROM a horrendous dream into a ghastly reality, my mind cloudy and heavy from the night before. Amarula, oh my goodness, the nectar of the gods. I remember sitting around the fire, drinking glass after glass. When I got up to use the bathroom, I stumbled a little and thought back to earlier in the day when our guide told us about the marula tree and the hard, little yellowish-brown fruits the tree produces. Christiaan went on to tell us the fruit ferments and becomes intoxicating. He explained that the animals find the sweet, succulent fruit irresistible, and they gorge themselves on the flesh and the fruit until they, too, become intoxicated. In particular, the monkeys eat so much and become so drunk that they fall out of the trees onto the ground below. In my own intoxicated state, I giggled.

"I'm a little monkey; I'm a little monkey," I murmured in a singsong voice on my way to the ladies' room.

But later, with the pounding headache and my stomach bile threatening to let loose at any moment—I was no longer finding it funny. The I'm-a-little-monkey chant got all mixed up with a shrieking that sounded both near and far away at the same time.

"She's gone! She's gone!" repeated over and over, my mind so befuddled I couldn't tell if I was dreaming or if someone was, indeed, screaming. No matter, either way, my thumping head retaliated in agony.

Soon there came a banging on the door, more like the shutters that served as a pseudobarrier between the rest of the world and me.

"Madam, madam, come please," the voice begged.

I rolled out of bed, struggling to stand upright. *Where the hell is David?*

The throbbing in my head had become only more intense as the moments ticked by. I could barely keep my stomach contents contained within my body. I staggered to the door in my flimsy pajamas. As I approached, the pounding on the shutters became only more insistent.

"What IS it?" I hissed as I pushed open the doors.

Akilah gasped, "Madam, Little Miss is gone!"

And that's when I lost it. I knew in an instant that she meant Hannah, and the stomach contents that refused to obey my will spewed all over the mahogany floor. Akilah grabbed me as I fell onto my knees in the midst of my own sick. My head felt as though it was going to burst wide open and my brains would splatter onto the floor if I made any noise at all. What began as a thin, high squeal gained momentum and turned into a full-fledged howl I didn't recognize as my own. My anguish came from the tips of my toes and racked my entire body.

Gone. Gone where?

None of this made any sense. Hannah followed the rules. She would never have gone off on her own and certainly not in the middle of the night. Who had taken her and why? Was her story of the three-year-old being kidnapped a premonition? Was that why she had shared the story?

The questions kept coming in a rapid-fire and wouldn't stop. Did I fail to see it and fail to understand it? Keeping her safe—of course, I had failed. If I hadn't drunk so much that night, I would have heard her, heard her moving around, heard the door, heard something.

Oh my god.

My stomach heaved again. What had happened to my baby? I didn't know if she was better off being kidnapped or better off wandering around the savannah.

Word spread quickly through the reserve. David had gone off early to set up for his next assignment. Did she go with him? There's no way he would have let her go with him. His work far too important to spend time being distracted by an eight-year-old, even if it was his own daughter. But maybe, a glimmer of hope, a sliver of possibility. But I knew in my heart that it wasn't so. My daughter had to be out there somewhere, somewhere on her own. Most definitely scared out of her mind. What was I going to do?

I don't know how long I remained down on the floor on my knees. It felt like an eternity, but I couldn't stay there. I had to find her. Akilah helped me up and led me over to our sitting area. She sat me down and made me a cup of steaming, thick, strong coffee. I didn't think I'd be able to keep it down, but my bigger problem was the physical act of drinking. My hands were shaking so badly that the ceramic cup kept banging against the saucer, and I was trembling so fiercely that the coffee sloshed over the sides as I tried to bring the cup to my mouth. Akilah took the cup and saucer from my hands and brought the cup to my lips. I sipped greedily, not caring if it would remain in my stomach.

BEFORE LONG, Christiaan visited our quarters. David wouldn't be back until tomorrow, and our situation required a knowledgeable leader. Christiaan had also grown up near to this exact camp. His father had been a guide. His grandfather, his great-grandfather, and his great-great-grandfather had all worked this land and had guided safaris as a form of supporting their families. Christiaan was of Dutch heritage; his lineage could be traced back to the first Dutch who were stranded on the Cape in 1647. Ever so grateful to see him, I beckoned him to join us and asked him if he'd like some coffee.

Damnit, Maggie, this isn't a social call; your daughter has gone missing. What is wrong with you?

Sensing my awkwardness, Christiaan sat on the chair facing me and politely solicited a cup of java from Akilah, who happily obliged.

Christiaan looked worried. Not that he wouldn't have been worried to begin with, but he looked terribly worried as if he were in physical pain.

"Maggie, I have absolutely no reason to believe that Hannah has been kidnapped."

I looked up into his face, and the instant our eyes met, we both knew what had happened. Hannah went off to comfort Numbalo in his time of death.

"What concerns me most are the conditions. Even in the best of times, with plenty of water and prey available, it would be a remarkable stretch to believe that Hannah would be untouched by the animals. But with the land as dry as it is and the water disappearing, the animals are becoming desperate. I don't say this to scare you, but you deserve to know the truth of what we are dealing with."

The tears spilled over my eyelids and down the sides of my face. I could feel them streaming as though there were channels running down either side of my face. Occasionally, my tongue flicked to the side to remove the moisture pooling there, and I could taste the salt of my own tears.

Christiaan continued, "I don't need to tell you, but your daughter is in grave danger."

My deepest, darkest fear had been realized. Hannah would have been better off if she had been kidnapped. At least then she'd have a chance.

THE TRUCKS ASSEMBLED in an astonishingly quick period of time—not only our trucks but the trucks from the neighboring reserves came as well. Christiaan was highly respected in these parts. He spoke the language. He was knowledgeable about the land and the animals. He worked the land and knew just as much as the staff who could trace their lineage back to the Khosian, the first tribe to ever inhabit this land more than one hundred thousand years ago. Christiaan was fair but not lax. He was good-humored but a leader in every sense of the word. Not only did all the drivers and guides assemble when he called, but cooks and housekeepers and other staff members from across the veld came to assist as well.

"Please let me come with you," I begged, but he would have nothing to do with it.

"I can't protect you and find Hannah at the same time. You must stay here and wait. If there's something you want to do, you would be best served by praying for our success and your daughter's safe return."

I melted into tears again, feeling as though this were all my fault and absolutely helpless to do anything about it. I had truly failed miserably this time—completely failed as a mother.

I remained numb while everyone around me and around the camp was brisk with activity and plans for locating Hannah. Christiaan kept telling me I couldn't go with him, that I must stay here. I had to convince him that I was meant to go, there was nothing I could do here except possibly hurt myself, and that I would go absolutely mad if I didn't feel like I was doing something.

"Look," I finally asked him, "What if David comes back early from his assignment; I cannot be here alone if he does."

Christiaan saw the sheer terror, fear, and desperation in my eyes, and he finally relented.

"Get dressed, and I'll meet you by the main gate in ten minutes. I need to give instructions to the rest of the crew."

I withdrew to the bathroom to pull myself together. The hangover had left, and in its place was an emptiness in the pit of my stomach, the emptiness and horrendously sick feeling I could not shake with the disappearance of Hannah.

What kind of a mother am I?

I have asked myself this question thousands of times before when I've messed up, but this was major league.

What kind of a mother am I? When did I become so pathetic? She deserves so much better. I have failed her in the worst possible way.

These thoughts were running through my mind as I ran a cool cloth over my face, neck, and hair. I passed the towel over my bare arms and legs and slipped into a tank top and cargo pants. I fumbled with the snaps, my hands shaking badly. I grabbed my pullover and daypack and headed out through the lodge. Akilah, God bless her, handed me a hot mug of tea, bowed her head, and wished us luck. I paced the entrance to the lodge, impatient that we hadn't started moving yet, but I could tell that Christiaan was methodical in the organization of the search party and was leaving nothing to chance. Despite my impatience, I was comforted briefly by his thoughtfulness and his command of this dire situation. Christiaan helped me into the truck and handed me a blanket. Moses was sitting shotgun on the front of the truck. This brought on a new wave of tears as I thought how entertaining it had been having him sit on this little perch affixed to the front of the truck with his shotgun while we were safe out riding around looking for animals. But this morning, it was exceedingly disconcerting when I thought of Hannah not safely sitting within the confines of the truck but rather on the other side. Ten other trucks joined us, lined up just outside the gates. Eleven in total, Hannah's favorite number; this must be a good sign. The women had prepared an astonishing amount of food for the men in such a short period of time. In just a few more minutes, we were finally off.

ALL MORNING, I swung madly between pure hope, my eyes darting fervently, my mind willing my eyes to see through the trees, to see through the brush to where my Hannah might be. I hovered on the edge of the bench, my heart light with optimism, rationalizing that she couldn't possibly have gotten very far and we were to come upon her at any moment. Scanning, scanning, straining to hear anything that might lead us to my sweet girl. And then I plunged into frantic despair, convinced that she was lost to me forever. The one thing that didn't falter was the tears; they just kept coming consciously and unconsciously. They had simply become a part of me, like my arms or my toes. There were unfamiliar voices on the radio in a language I couldn't understand. I didn't even understand Christiaan when he spoke over the line.

We had been out all day, and the sun was beginning to set. Christiaan insisted on taking me back to camp, and this time I agreed. He promised me that he and his men would return to the search, but first, they needed a break and to replenish supplies. Although mournful that the efforts today had failed to locate Hannah, I marveled at the glorious African sunset. I had never witnessed such beauty in my life. The sky came alive and ablaze with the most shocking shades of red, orange, and yellow. It was as if the sky was self-destructing in the most splendid offering and sacrifice to bring forth the following day that waited to be birthed. Similar to the way I felt annihilated inside, yet I couldn't help but appreciate this gift, this wondrous miracle that comes to pass each and every day, and my hopes of finding Hannah were restored.

DAVID RETURNED the next day, as expected. He was informed of the previous day's events before he ever made it to our rooms. Shortly before he arrived, Akilah had offered to make me a cup of tea. When she arrived with the tea in hand, he ordered her to leave.

"Leave, woman. She doesn't deserve your pity or your kindness."

I agreed. At this moment, I didn't feel like I deserved

anything at all, anything except the misery and grief growing exponentially inside of myself. David was engulfed with anguish, and as that subsided, he was overcome with fury. Christiaan did his best to calm him down long enough to listen, and I began to inform David of our suspicions.

"Let's forget for a moment the preposterousness that she could even approach an animal without being killed, but to think that she could actually help them—a lion! You're stupider than you look."

I flushed with embarrassment at Christiaan witnessing this interaction between my husband and myself. Instantaneously, I felt like I had felt my whole life when someone criticized me or if I even detected a hint of disapproval. I, Maggie, as a human, was just wrong. I had let countless relationships and interactions dictate my worth and value. I would never measure up; I believed this wholeheartedly. I had been told a million different times and a million different ways how I was wrong, and I believed each and every one of them.

"Sir, I know it sounds outrageous, but your daughter seems to have something, some kind of connection with these animals that I can't explain. I have been a guide here for thirty-some years and my father and his father and his father before that never, in all our hundreds of thousands of rides, have the animals behaved in the manner they did in her presence."

"What manner?" David demanded.

"They have always allowed us to come close," Christiaan continued, "but they have never approached the vehicles before. They have never shown themselves in this fashion before. They've never prostrated themselves before the vehicles and shown any curiosity or interest in us before unless it was with aggression. This has been just the opposite, far from aggression. It has been almost like a beckoning or an invitation to join them."

"Oh, this is rich," David replied. "You are just as delusional as she is. Where am I going to locate someone competent who will find her?"

"I don't want to spread false hope, sir, but the fact remains, we have yet to find a body, and the animals here don't hide their prey. They gorge on it in the open. Surely, if she had been killed, we would have found her already."

"What you are suggesting is completely ridiculous."

I went to touch David, as much for his comfort as my own. He shook my hand off like a wet dog.

From between his teeth, he hissed, "How dare you? How dare you come to me after losing our daughter, you stupid, drunken fool."

So, there it was, the words that described exactly what he thought of me—no comfort to be had between us at all. Any pretense of love, all my disillusioned hopes for this marriage were smashed to pieces out in the open. There'd be no recovering from this point going forward.

This was now the established order.

GETTING TO WORK with David excited me, but having him choose me, pick me to be with, thrilled me beyond my wildest imagination. He was so, so perfect. Everyone who met him loved him. He was a man's man and could charm any woman. I loved going to new places with him and experiencing a whole new side of our city and the world I had never experienced before. I loved it when we were going on a date, my days filled with joyful anticipation and dreams. I would envision what I was going to change into for the evening ahead; I would spend extra time on my make-up and hair. I wanted to be perfect for him. On one of our first dates, he took me to a high-end seafood place. I didn't eat seafood, but I figured they always have at least one option for us land lovers. I left work early so I could be ready on time. As we drove in David's luxurious car to the restaurant, he held my hand. I believed myself to be in a dream, floating along in this beautiful car, with this beautiful man, off to eat some beautiful food. Like so many things he'd introduced me to, I had never encountered anything like this before. David was so attentive and caring. He helped me from the car, he held doors open for me, and he had me lead the way when it was time to be seated. I felt like a fairy princess. I couldn't think of a time when I had ever been romanced before. With David's impressive command of the wine list, he ordered something that sounded rather special and tasted even better. Our waiter could not have been finer; he tended to us in an extremely solicitous manner without being obnoxious or intrusive. I'm pretty sure I saw David raise an eyebrow when I ordered a steak, but the moment passed so quickly I couldn't be sure. I had a terrific evening, one that I built a whole lot of hopes and dreams upon.

After that night, between work and dates, I saw or spoke to David nearly every day. When we weren't together, he sent flirty texts and called to see how I was doing. A few days prior to the opening of David's show, he asked me if I liked to play golf.

"Oh, I'm terrible at it, but I'd love to learn."

Who the hell just said that?

I hate golf; I couldn't believe those words had just come out of my mouth. But David seemed thoroughly pleased, so I decided to just let it go. The next morning when I arrived at the gallery, David grabbed my hand and took me out to the parking garage. He informed me we were taking the day off to go play golf. I had a look of utter shock and bewilderment when we got to his car and he opened the trunk. He had purchased me a full set of brand-new clubs and shoes, and he handed me a gift box to unwrap that I could only assume had a golf outfit inside of it.

"Don't worry. It's going to be a wonderful day," he reassured as he opened the passenger door for me. I smiled as graciously as I could as I got into the car. When he closed the door, I suddenly felt as though the car transformed into a coffin and I was suffocating.

THE DAYS WENT BY slower than molasses with no news of Hannah. David held Akilah at bay and kept me sequestered in our rooms. The sadness became too much to bear. The only relief came when I took a drink. I tried not to, but it was the only lifeline I had. I'd resolve not to take another drink, but then my resolution would vanish. David would mock and taunt me, but at this point, I was much too destroyed to even care. I deserved this punishment for failing the one person I loved more than anyone in the world, myself included. The grief overtook virtually every cell of my body. I was restless, yet I could not move. My mind would not shut down its own hatred unless soothed with a drink. I'd been abandoned by life. My skin felt as though it had been turned inside out and set aflame. At night, the unrelenting voices came, the restlessness caused my body to toss and turn, trying to find an answer where there was none. My chest had been ripped apart, my heart cracked open and left there to bleed, to become infected with anything the world had to throw at me. I missed Hannah more than I ever thought possible. I suffered in so much pain, and yet somehow, each morning, I continued to wake.

The ominous mist around the camp remained, but the roaring had stopped. This silence was crippling. I didn't realize it at the moment, but somehow the sound of the lion's roar in the night had been a comfort to me. It connected me to Hannah, to her brilliance both inside and out. It stoked what little hope I had within. The silence left behind was another crushing loss, leaving with it a pain that pierced my bones in a way that made me want to rip them from my own body. How would I ever continue on without knowing what had happened to Hannah? I am an optimist at my core, but as the days passed, I had to believe she was dead. I don't know if it was stupidity or denial, but I just couldn't reconcile the fact she was truly gone forever with the tiny flickering flame of hope inside that I could not extinguish. Yet, I could not deny the fact that she had been gone far too long to have survived even though we had not been able to find any evidence of her death. I didn't want to go on without her; maybe that was my answer.

That morning, David reached over to me and wrapped his arm above my waist beneath my breasts in anticipation of having sex. I couldn't endure it that morning. My whole body froze. I hoped he didn't feel it, but how could he not? The last thing I wanted to do right then was have sex. I had been yearning for David to touch me in some shape of compassion since the day Hannah disappeared, and here it was, but not like this. I rolled onto my side, and when I did, he started to grind his hardness into my backside.

"I'm sorry. I can't," I implored.

David threw back the covers and practically leaped out of bed. "What do you mean you can't? You can't? Well, then who the hell can?"

As much as I willed them away, the tears started to come in a torrent, streaming down my cheeks. "You don't get it. She is all I ever had. I am nothing without her."

"Ha," he scoffed, "you are nothing, period." He whipped on the pants that he had laid on the floor beside the bed, snatched his jacket off the chair in the seating area, and stormed out.

AFTER SEVERAL DAYS, while David had left on assignment, Akilah came to see me. Although there was alarm in her eyes when she first saw me, that shifted to compassion as she found me lying across the bed. Unwashed for weeks now, my mouth was crusted over and my hair a tangled mess. I reeked of alcohol, filth, and despair. Quickly, she ran to the bathroom and started the tub. Gingerly, she lifted my arms and began to guide me toward the tub. I resisted her.

"David is coming back. He will find you here. You must leave," I pleaded.

"Not until you are washed." She helped me into the bath and proceeded to wash me as one would wash a little baby.

It was with such tenderness and loving hands, I thought I might simply dissolve under her touch. She started at my neck, face, and mouth and wiped away the crust that had been lingering there for far too long. She lifted each arm with the warmheartedness of a mother. As she washed up and down the length of my arm, I couldn't help but notice the contrast of her dark skin, which seemed so strong compared to my delicate white skin that could peel away at any moment. She pitched the top half of my limp body forward in order to scrub my back. I could feel the suds from the sponge trickle down my spine into the water below. She shifted my body back against the rear of the tub so she could cleanse my chest. Her sponge moved across my skin in small circles as she moved across my collarbone and down to my breasts. I could feel her devotion to this bath as the ultimate blessing from one mother to another. All the while, she half-hummed, half-sang songs in a lilting, listful melody. I found my fear dissipating under her skillful and loving hands. I began to relax for the first time since Hannah's disappearance. She started to wash my hair, promising to restore it to its former glory.

I snorted at this, and she replied, "No, madam, you are exquisite. You have wonderful gifts that God has given you, and one of them is great beauty. You are a warrior mama with great strength and intelligence. You are a beacon of light for the souls all around you. You just don't recognize it in yourself. And once you do, your daughter will return to you."

I let her words wash over me just like the water I steeped in, and I began to weep. Never in my life had someone cared for me, touched me with such unconditional love like Akilah had in that moment. I never wanted it to end.

WE BOTH HEARD it at the same time: David's return. He showed up more than a day early, but we heard the undeniable squeak of the door to our dwelling as it swung open.

Enraged, David entered the sanctuary of the bathroom. He practically threw Akilah out of the hut, grabbing her by the shoulders and shaking her violently as he dragged her out.

My tears of joy turned into tears of panic and outrage as I shouted and pleaded for him to leave her alone.

"You're next," he spewed over his shoulder at me.

Oh god, I was so weak. I had to will myself out of the bath. It felt like an eternity, but it could only have been moments. I grabbed the nearest towel to cover myself. I didn't know where to go. I headed into the bedroom to get some clothes, and David returned from the front door at the same time.

"Who do you think you are?" he shouted from the entry to the bedroom.

"I, I just, just..." I stammered, trying so hard to make any sense of what was happening and finding none. I had never seen David so angry, ever, and I was truly frightened as he came closer. I skittered around the bed as he lunged for me while I darted toward the door. He caught me by the hair. The towel, all but forgotten, fell to the floor. I don't even recall it happening. My whole world was falling apart. My daughter was missing, and the man I had once loved had turned into a demon of the worst sort.

He had me by the hair, and as he whispered, "Not so fast, sweetheart," he threw me onto the bed. I was so weak I could not fight. I was mentally weak and physically weak, and at this point, I just gave up, face down on the bed while David straddled on top of me. He pressed my face into the mattress. I could hear the click-click as he undid his belt buckle and the ripping sound as he undid the zipper of his pants and the sound of his pants against his skin as he removed them.

I had never felt more helpless and more afraid, a flash of the impala up in the tree came into my head. This man who I had been naked with thousands of times was scaring the daylights out of me. He lifted my hip with one hand, and with the other, jammed himself inside of me. I screamed out in pain as he entered me. It felt as though I would split in two. I screamed out as much in pain as I did for the loss of this relationship, for which I had always held out a desperate hope. With each thrust, the insults kept coming, each with a rhythm of their own.

"You dirty bitch. You rotten, no-good cunt. You are worthless to me now and always have been," over and over again.

Knowing full well how outrageous this behavior was, I still felt as though somehow I deserved it. Somehow, I had brought this on upon myself and this was my lot in life. He finally came and withdrew himself. He pulled my hair and shoved my face back into the pillow.

He slapped my ass and taunted, "Here's looking at you, kid."

The tears had never stopped. I didn't think it possible that I had any left in me, but they kept coming. My nose ran, and its substance smeared all over my face. My hair had fallen into my eyes, and my whole body felt like it had betrayed me, simply by just being.

At some point, while I lay there, David left our rooms. I had failed again, failed miserably as a wife, and failed even more miserably as a mom. Didn't anyone get it? This is all I was. It was all I had, and now I was left with nothing.

I was nothing.

AFTER A WHILE, Akilah came and helped me get dressed. Again with her loving arms, Akilah slipped my clothes over my battered body and smoothed my bruised mind and ego with her words and her songs. She brought me to the kitchen so she could watch over me while she and the others prepared the evening meal. Every once in a while, she would bring over a little dish of their preparations for me to taste. She brought me a cup of tea and patted my hand.

Behatti played nearby, and I noticed that she had Hannah's American Girl doll with her. I motioned for her to come closer, and she did so hesitantly, for she thought she was in trouble. I invited her onto my lap and held her tightly. I missed Hannah so much, it was unbearable. I shared with Behatti how Hannah loved this little dolly. Despising the materialism attached to these particular dolls, it was something neither her dad nor I would ever have bought for her, but she came up with ways to earn money and saved up for the purchase herself. I told Behatti about the bed Hannah and her father had built for Dolly and how she would sing to her and cradle her, and I broke down into sobs.

"Yes, madam," Behatti answered. "Hannah give me," and she lifted the doll to my face and gave her a little squeeze.

"Wait, what? Hannah intended to go away?"

"Yes, madam," Behatti said, eyes downcast in barely a whisper.

"Akilah, where's Christiaan?" Poor little Behatti nearly toppled over as I jumped to my feet and reached out my arm to steady her.

My heart beat wildly as I frantically grabbed Akilah and insisted, "Hannah left on purpose; she wasn't taken. I knew it! But why would she leave?

Why would she—that lion, it must be—she did go to help that lion. Oh my god, she must still be out there, she must be waiting for me, she must—I deflated as I grasped the chances of her still being alive were one in a million.

DAVID RETURNED LATE that evening, behaving as though nothing had taken place between us. I looked at him, flabbergasted at how he could possibly think we could carry on as though nothing had happened.

"Maggie, pack the bags. We are leaving this shithole first thing in the morning."

I scrambled off the sofa, and as I opened the suitcase laid across the bed, I started to shake.

Every fiber of my being convulsed with rage as I let out a roar, "No! I will NOT pack the bags. I will NOT leave this 'shithole.' I'm not going anywhere with you, David. It's over. I'm done. Pack your own goddamn bag."

"Don't you dare threaten me, Maggie. I guarantee you will not like the results."

"David," I asserted with surprising calmness and strength, "there is nothing further you can do to hurt me. I have nothing left for you to take from me. I do not want to be married to you any longer, and you will be leaving on your own."

"You will regret this, Maggie. I promise you that. When I walk out that door, there is no going back."

"Just go," I groaned, slowly shaking my head from side to side.

I LEFT THE HUT and hid myself away in the camp library. I had no desire to hang around for more insults or abuse while David packed up to leave. It had taken the cruelest of acts for me to finally recognize that I would never be enough for David. I had been plagued with anxiety trying to guess and gauge every mood, every whim, every outburst of his. No matter how hard I tried, it would never be enough. I couldn't think of a worse time to try and extricate myself from this relationship, but for some strange reason in the depths of my soul, I knew if I were to get out of this alive, it needed to happen right then. The thought of putting an end to our marriage made me inexplicably sad. I hoped for so much when I met David. I'd had such simple dreams about how and what our life would be like.

I must be crazy, I considered, to still have these kinds of feelings after all that I had just been through. But even after all of that, I still felt guilty that somehow, someway, it was my fault for not being enough—a belief that had tormented me since I was a young girl, never being enough. I wished he could see and accept me for who I was, and I felt guilty for pretending for so long.

I would never be able to love him enough, be enough for him, or do enough for him. I had finally stood up for myself, finally put an end to the abuse that I had endured for far too long. Although I did not delude myself into thinking all would be well, I had taken that critical first step. I still needed to dig myself out of this immeasurable hole if I were ever to reclaim my own life. I was strong enough to confront David, and now it was time to confront myself. I had finally shattered the illusion of the life I was living and began to crack open my truth.

I would have to make some rather radical changes, for one—no more drinking. Wow, for the first time, that thought didn't send my brain and body into panic mode. It no longer sounded like a threat or a punishment; it simply felt like my next logical step. Unlike the thousands of times before when I had sworn off drinking forever, this time I thought I could actually do it.

My mantra became, "Let's see how it goes today, and tomorrow we'll start again."

EVERYTHING FELT all mixed up, and there were mornings I awoke and didn't know if I could make it through the day. The loss of Hannah, the end of my marriage—I had no clue who I was or where I was to go from here. I had stashed Hannah's bag in the corner, and I pulled it out to start my daily ritual, although today it was without a cocktail nearby. As I sat on the floor, I drew the bag close. I pulled out each and every item we had packed for the trip. Every article of clothing went into a pile. I held each item in my hands and pressed it against my face, breathing deeply as if I could breathe life into these clothes and conjure her before me. I held them out in front of me and inspected them. Her favorite unicorn dress, the white long-sleeved shirt she wore over on the plane with red stains down the front from where she dribbled Jell-O all over herself. Each time, I thought how ridiculous it was for an airline to serve kids red Jell-O. And each time I gazed at it, it made me laugh as I saw myself looking over at her when it happened and the precious expression on her face when she looked back at me and blurted, "Uh-oh."

There's the grown-up sweater wrap that I bought her

specifically for this trip; she fell in love with this wrap. Her nightgown splashed with silly gnomes. After I refolded her clothes and returned them to the bag, I started to add her toothbrush, hairbrush, her favorite mystery book, her diary. Yet, this time I hesitated and set the diary aside. There's nothing of significance in it. We had all looked, but I thought that if I write in it too, I'd feel closer to her somehow. I packed up the bag and placed it back into the corner. I set the diary onto the table near the bed and decide I will write in it later.

As the days slipped by, I discovered writing in Hannah's journal to be remarkably therapeutic. As part of my recovery, I would have to forgive myself for all the horrible lies I told myself and all the awful things I did to myself. I started with this.

Dear Maggie,

You have traveled a hard road, and yes, it is because of your choosing. Your drinking has shaped the situation you find yourself in right now. You've allowed others to influence and decide your state, your being, who you want to be in this world. It is turning a blind eye and letting others take the lead in your life. Being fooled into thinking that control was love.

Your family, your husband. It has been easier on the surface to not have to fight, to just surrender instead of always having to protect, easier to submit and keep the peace. And at what cost? The cost of dying inside and wanting to die—to just make it stop—just make the pain stop and go away. The pain of trying to protect your child from it all.

Hannah, sweet Hannah, where have you gone? What were you thinking, going off on your own to help Numbalo? This is the only logical thing that could have taken you away from me. I want to be angry with you. I want to ask you how you could be so careless. But you, Hannah, have always been so extraordinary, I almost understand why you left. I only wish I could have protected you from whatever fate befell you.

The searching has stopped from an organized standpoint, although Christiaan and I still search frequently with no luck. I don't know that I will ever stop searching for you, my love, seeing your face in the child of a guest, hearing your voice in another's laughter. I do know I never have to search for you in my heart—you are always right there.

I know that I must go on without you. I must move forward, or I will go mad. I couldn't protect you from your father's tirades, but I know now that you saw right through him, you understood his nature much more than I did. I endured so much for so long that I see I got lost in the pain.

Criticize, criticize, criticize, and the accolades are piecemealed out like little pellets to a rat. These pellets from David have been extremely seductive—just enough to keep you around pleasing, doing, hoping for any little scrap of recognition, any little scrap of love. This repeated pattern you've kept silent about because you didn't want to admit the truth and acknowledge it and then feel as though you were required to do something about it—like leave. You were scared of that change; you were scared to leave.

Toying with you on a whim. Bullying, slave and master, wielding malicious words like a sword to crucify you if you got too—? Got too what? Independent? Self-sufficient? Is that where his other wives were? Were they relieved to let him go, as you are relieved now? Is that why none of them put up a fight?

How do you move forward from this? You are growing stronger as you become aware of the detrimental influences you have been under. Being oblivious to these forces has afforded you some wonderful material things and experiences, experiences you have grown from and that have expanded your mind and your being. You are awakening to acceptance, combined with times of denial—there is no immediate rush— you are strong enough to keep yourself out of danger. You will learn more; you will continue to grow and expand with other experiences and relationships you attract into your life from this healthier state. You are whole, you are a beautiful soul, and there are so many who love you and appreciate you for everything that you are and everything you want to be.

I forgive you for everything that you feel guilty for, for everything you "think" you've done wrong—for everyone you feel that you have hurt. This is not about making amends or reparations—it's about moving on, moving forward from this point where you are right now. What are you going to do with all these lessons? How are you going to show up? Who are you going to be? You need not be difficult on yourself. I know things can be hard, but you make them so much harder sometimes, harder than they have to be. Whatever happens from this point forward, you will be more than OK.

AKILAH HAD ANOTHER wonderful daughter, Corlia. She was significantly older than Behatti, but by how much, I did not know. She stood taller than her mother and a few shades darker. Her hair was closely cropped, and instead of wearing a full *doek*, she opted for thick headbands in fanciful colors. Her cheekbones were high and well-defined. She carried a solemn expression, yet her laugh was infectious, and I often found myself cheerful around her despite my dire circumstances. Corlia was expecting her own child, and her pregnancy had been causing her some problems. She experienced sickness more often than not, and when the day came that she could no longer work in the reserve gift shop, Akilah came to me.

"Madam, I would never impose upon you, but we are in a bind, and although I know it is way beneath you, will you be willing to look after the gift shop while Corlia is out?"

I hesitated. I didn't know the money here. *What if I messed up?* I knew the items in the gift shop were a result of extensive hard labor, and what if I couldn't do it? Akilah mistook my hesitation for disgust; she semi-bowed and backed away, apologizing profusely for disturbing and insulting me.

"No, wait!" I finally managed to blurt out. "I would be delighted to help in the gift shop. I just don't know how."

"Oh, madam, it is easy. I will show you. We go now." I lifted myself off the chair and followed Akilah to the gift shop. I hadn't been in it since the day we arrived. I remembered the visual feast my eyes took in from all of the unique handmade crafts. We arrived, and Akilah unlocked the door and gestured for me to go first. It was larger than I remembered. I suppose that's because I'd been confined to our lodging since Hannah disappeared.

Exquisiteness touched every space of this little shop. No time to admire that now, but there would be plenty of time for that later. Akilah showed me the little cash register, the receipt books, and the slips to fill out for a room charge. It all seemed quite straightforward, and I was not nearly as fearful and uncertain as I had been twenty minutes prior. I tingled with appreciation to finally have something to do with myself, something to think about other than my missing daughter and my dead marriage.

WRITING IN HANNAH'S DIARY somehow made me feel closer to her. I would lose myself for just a few moments and could pretend life was normal and my little girl would be skipping through the door at any moment. But all it would take was a far-off noise or the sound of something emitted through the camp, and I got yanked back into the crushing reality that I was here. All alone. My daughter's disappearance was still a mystery, and David was physically gone for good, although his mental and energetic presence still haunted me with its oppressiveness and the weight of his accusations. I tossed the journal aside with disgust, feeling foolish for thinking, dreaming, hoping that I could escape this never-ending nightmare only to pick it up the next night and the next, desperate for respite from the pain, even if it was only for a few minutes of delusional hope. I wanted to run and hide, but something kept me anchored to this very spot. I must feel this pain, be a witness to my pain—a pain that had taken on a life of its own. It was uncomplicated before, just the promise of a drink would help my pain subside. It was simple back then to take that next drink and the next until my pain obliterated in my own numbness. But the repercussions of that numbness had left me numb to life, numb to myself, and numb to everything that was happening around me. Now I would not take that drink. I would have to confront this pain, feel it full-on, and come out the other side before I would find any relief.

Day after day, I warred with my mind. My heart and soul as a mother would not believe that my Hannah was gone for good, but my mind persisted in its message for me to accept the horrible truth that Hannah was dead. At times like this, times when my mind would win, I became crippled with anguish and the blood drained from my body until I felt completely apathetic, completely void of hope and completely void of pain in the same breath, which in and of itself was more excruciating than any being should have to bear. I didn't remember actually going to bed or falling asleep. I did remember the crushing disappointment I felt that I was still alive when I awoke. I had to wait until my breath found me again. Not only was Hannah still gone, but I lived in fear and suspense as if David were still my husband and he would come raging into my room like he did not so long ago. I begged for God to please just take me and put me out of my misery. But I lingered there whether I liked it or not. I closed my eyes, willing myself back to sleep, but my efforts were futile.

AFTER WHAT FELT LIKE another lifetime of being on my own, I was able to pull myself together and regain some semblance of normalcy. I washed on a somewhat regular basis, and with Akilah's aid began to put the meager pieces of my life back together. I did not know if I would ever see Hannah again. She obviously had yet to be found alive or dead, and I remained here, still flesh and blood with a heart that continued to beat despite all my desires to make it stop.

I had a life before David, before Hannah in particular, but having a taste of life in the world with her in it and then to have her snatched away was not a world worth being in. But here I stayed, Maggie, no longer a wife and no longer a mother. Maggie, in all her despicable glory, who had no business standing here before anybody or anything and for whatever godforsaken reason must pick up the pieces and move on. Move on to what or where? I had no fucking idea. But I did believe in the grand design of the universe, and there had to be a reason I was left standing even as meekly as I stood there at that moment. Writing in Hannah's journal had become integral to my healing process. I had lost my only source of happiness, and I knew I had to reclaim this happiness and wholeness within myself. As I mindlessly wrote on the pages of Hannah's diary, I found I had formulated a letter to David, a letter to David that he would never see, that I would never send, but I am astonished at the words I had written.

Dear David,

I expected too much from you.

I came to you as a broken woman with the faulty expectation that you could fix me, you couldn't. It was unfair of me to expect and demand that you do.

Now I know that I was never truly broken—just wounded, and I was the only person with the power to do that healing. I needed to heal myself and take responsibility for my own wounds.

I was so angry because you never behaved the way I wanted you to behave. You never behaved the way I expected you to behave. I never should have put those kinds of expectations on you.

I am shocked by your coldheartedness over losing our daughter, Hannah, and how easy it was for you to just pick up and leave.

The last time we were together, you scared me and

hurt me. I want to forgive you, but it is not my place to forgive you; it is God's.

I will never understand or comprehend what came over you, but I know in order to move on, I must acknowledge and feel the devastation of what happened between us and release it.

And I need to release you too, David. I know I told you I didn't want to be married anymore, and we will be divorced, but I need to release you emotionally as well. I stood up to you the night you left, and I am standing up to you here.

It was NOT OK for you to abandon Hannah.

It was NOT OK for you to criticize me and blame me for things that went wrong.

It was NOT OK for you to piecemeal out your affection like tiny pellets to a rat.

It was NOT OK for you to bully me and tear me down.

It was NOT OK for you to sabotage the efforts I made toward my dream.

It was NOT OK for you to mock and belittle me.

It was NOT OK for you to ignore me.

Now that I am clear and no longer drinking, I can see this truth, our truth, and own my part in creating *this truth. And because I created it, I can change it. And I choose to change it now.*

Goodbye, David. Goodbye.

A feeling of finality and acceptance had washed over me. It was hugely liberating to emotionally shut this door on David, and the acceptance I felt was more about Hannah and the awful tragedy that must have become of her—the acceptance that even if she never came back to me, I might, just might, be able to find some happiness and healing deep within me.

I leaped from the bed and danced ecstatically as if I were possessed. No music, no beat for me to follow, no beat other than the beat of my own heart, which was highly erratic, pounding through my body like the surprising beat of the African drums I had heard night after night while dinner preparations were being made. I shouted out unintelligible sounds and words. I threw my head back and cackled like a lunatic. I sounded as though I was speaking in tongues. Akilah knocked on my door and didn't wait for a reply before she entered. Clearly alarmed at my behavior, she thought I had gone mad. I grabbed her hands and spun her around in circles, and soon she was whooping and dancing just as crazily as me. We both flopped onto the bed in the center of the room and gazed up at the teak paneled ceiling with its great, giant fan spinning 'round and 'round, the same as we just were.

We caught our breath, and I shouted out loud, "I'm free!"

I felt less sad for the first time since Hannah's disappearance. Akilah arose from the bed and placed her hands onto her hips.

Shaking her head at me, she clucked, "It's about damn time, madam!" and she took her leave.

My laughter trailed her out the door. My tormenting grief gave way to an inner wisdom that I was stronger than I had ever given myself credit for. The healing had finally taken root.

RAW THE NEXT MORNING, the euphoria of freedom had depleted most of my reserves. I did feel lighter somehow; I think it was the first morning I didn't curse God for keeping me alive. I still hurt, and there most definitely remained a huge space of emptiness and sorrow where Hannah should be. I couldn't imagine myself going home now. I couldn't leave until I knew for sure what had become of my sweet Hannah—an easy position for me to take, as there was nothing waiting for me at home. Plenty of money existed in my investment accounts for me to stay as long as I liked. The dazzling African landscape, with its equally captivating people and animals, was a balm for my soul, a reason to go on, a reason to heal myself back to whole.

I washed my face and ran a brush through my hair. I went to fetch something out of the wardrobe to wear and in place of the dirty, tired clothes that had become my weary uniform were three gaily colored saris, just like the ones the women in camp wore. I stared in astonishment, and I was wracked with gratitude to Akilah; this had to be her doing. I slipped the first one over my head, and it fit perfectly. The dress had a bold pattern of royal blue, navy blue, and gold in a horizontal sunburst pattern. The blues matched my eyes. The short sleeves and modest neckline were banded in black fabric with three buttons down the center of my chest. The long dress just skimmed my ankles. She even included a head wrap for me to tie my hair up into. It was one of the most simple and attractive garments I'd ever seen. I felt so cherished, replenished, and purposeful in my new uniform. How could she have known? Akilah held me at times when I couldn't hold myself; she was my guardian angel and best friend.

I took another long look in the mirror, and this time saw myself with some appreciation. My caramel-colored hair just barely grazed my shoulders, the fineness of it causing it to flutter in the mild breeze coming in from the window. Life without alcohol had allowed the excess pounds to lift from my frame, leaving me with a healthy shape. My skin had turned a darker shade; I could maybe pass for Italian instead of English. I'd always wanted to be Italian. What surprised me most of all about my appearance was the look of resolve I saw in my eyes, and when I took in this figure before me as a whole, I had to smile. The woman facing me was so beautiful, my eyes brimmed with tears. With a final glance in the mirror, I practically floated to the community kitchen.

I HAD FALLEN INTO a routine at the camp. I woke early to help the women prepare in the kitchen. The grunt work fell to me, but it didn't matter. Being an outsider, it took a long while for the women to even acknowledge my presence in the kitchen. I needed something to do, anything that kept my hands and my mind occupied. I chopped. I cleaned. I carried. None of it was beneath me. I had no right to be here, and I frantically wanted to remain in their company, so I was grateful for any task put before me. After morning preparations were done, I headed over to the gift shop. It could be dangerous for me if I was alone with my thoughts too much. Similar to my ritual with Hannah's belongings, I tenderly and lovingly addressed each item in the shop on any given day. I held it, dusted it, wiped it down, adjusted it on display just so. Each crafted item was remarkable, and as I slowly learned each woman's story behind these appealing creations, I revered them even more.

The shop closed from one to three o'clock to allow for lunch for the staff. I certainly didn't need two hours for lunch, so after a quick bite in the kitchen, it became customary for the children and myself to gather behind the kitchen for a quick lesson in English. The holidays were a particularly joyful time at the lodge, as the families of the staff were here to visit. It must be so difficult for the staff members to be away from their families for weeks on end, but these were prized jobs, and they considered themselves extremely fortunate for the ability to work at a camp and earn consistent money to help support their immediate and extended families. The staff village teemed with children of all ages, and they were all welcome to our open-air makeshift classroom, which consisted of a few tree stumps, a dirt floor, sticks for drawing pictures and letters in the dust, and some nearby trees that offered a canopy of shade and a few degrees of relief from the driving heat. These children were precious, absolutely precious. Their deep, creamy, rich brown skin provided a stark contrast in color to that of Hannah's milky-white skin. The boys all had thick, closely cropped wooly black hair that made me think of a ground cover we had at home. Its name escaped me. The girls wore their hair either cropped as well or in tight little braids. They dressed in clothes remarkably similar to those found in the states. One little boy wore a Nemo T-shirt nearly every day. There wasn't a movie theatre within hundreds of miles, yet Disney had, indeed, found its way here.

These English lessons first began with just Behatti and me playing around behind the kitchen while her mother worked. I'd teach her a word or two of English, and she, in exchange, would teach me the same word in her language. Soon, she started bringing some friends, and the women working in the kitchen encouraged their children to come as well. I knew there were a few eyebrows raised at the lodge—on both sides. Who does this white lady think she is? But, miraculously, I had stopped caring about what other people thought of me. The so-called appearances I'd been required to maintain throughout my life were of no further consequence. I was doing no harm, and without my Hannah nearby—who I missed desperately—being with these children eased some of my desperation and slightly filled the gaping hole in my soul. It was a bit of a double-edged sword since their presence magnified Hannah's absence, but I had too much love to share to keep it locked up inside.

Most were shy at first. They were so curious about me, curious about the woman who had lost her child. The timidity didn't last long as they were eager to show off the English they already knew. I laughed at the phases they had picked up, and our entire bitty group went into hysterics when one angelic little boy stood in front of me to share what he knew and began with, "Shit, shit, shit, motherfucker."

Yes, this fix was precisely what I needed.

After my time with the children, a few of them walked me to the gift shop and waved goodbye, hugs and kisses all around. I had grown so fond of these children, and as I squeezed each one, I felt such love and thankfulness for their existence in my life, my heart beat faster, and there was so much I wanted to say to them, so much I wanted them to know, but I simply held their tiny hands as we pulled away and smiled at each other.

AKILAH CAME IN to find me prostrate on the bed in my underpants on top of the covers. I couldn't even lift my head to acknowledge her arrival. She spotted Hannah's journal on the floor, and as she gently opened it, it fell to the last letter I had just written. She sat upon the floor and began to read.

"My dearest Hannah."

The tears fell from her eyes as she read the letter aloud. When she finished, she pulled the covers over my bare body and held me tightly. After a period of time, she arose and went to the sideboard to make us some tea.

"Tell me more about Hannah," she asked.

I opened my mouth to speak, but nothing came out. I choked on my own breath.

"Tell me what she was like when she wanted something; our little girls are always wanting something."

I began again, and my voice found me. As I started to share more about Hannah, I pulled on my robe and joined Akilah on the undersized sofa. Before I knew it, we were both laughing at the silly and wonderful things our daughters do. We've lived half a world apart, and yet the love and admiration for these exquisite young beings and our experiences as mothers were the same. The tears were still flowing, but they were tears of remembrance, tears of release, and tears of pure, untainted love.

If anyone saw us sitting there, they would think we were lifelong friends sharing a cup of tea and our deepest truths. I was beyond grateful for Akilah. I took her hands in mine and told her so.

WITH AKILAH'S HELP, I persuaded more and more women of her community and others close by to share their wares in the gift shop. The talent that lies within these extraordinary women astounded me. These gifts had been handed down over so many generations with no written record of it—gorgeous scarves, paintings, woven baskets with intricate designs and playful color combinations, beaded jewelry, pottery. Over time, I realized the women were coming to me for advice on how to price their goods. These women did not recognize the worth, the value, the splendor in their gifts. How could they not see it? They were humble and self-deprecating when they brought their

goods forth. Every time I exclaimed in delight, their embarrassment grew.

One young woman, in particular, was my favorite. She
had been disfigured in the sense that she had many burns
over her body. The burns on her face caused her right eye
to be shielded by scar tissue. Akilah recounted the day
Maia had received these horrendous injuries. Her husband
had a handful of friends over—they were all drinking. As
Maia refilled the men's glasses, one of them reached out
and grabbed her breast. Seeing this, her husband ordered
everyone out of the hut and tethered Maia and her four
children inside. Then he set the hut ablaze, intending to
burn all five of them alive. Akilah described the screaming
as unbearable, the sheer terror and savage atrocity, but as
her husband was regarded as a leader in their community,
everyone else remained indoors and figured that she and
her children had it coming to them.

By some miracle of God, the heavens opened up, and the
rain fell from the sky in torrents, extinguishing the deadly
flames. But not before Maia had sustained severe injuries.
Her children walked away with no visible scars, all but
the youngest, who perished several days later from smoke
inhalation. Maybe this explained my invisible connection
to this woman, for she, too, had experienced the loss of a

beloved child. Her left eye, the most stunning eye I had ever seen, reminded me of Hannah's. Its dominant amber color drew you into her gaze, and within it, I could identify flecks of every color of the rainbow. There were also rays of gold within her eye, and the articles she brought for the gift shop were truly exceptional. Hannah was continually in my thoughts, and although I was wounded myself, I knew that if I was going to survive without her, I would have to keep taking that next step.

BEFORE I MET DAVID, I worked in an art gallery. I didn't know a lot about art when I started, but I was a quick study and had a good eye for arrangement and what pieces complemented each other. Before long, I was tasked with curating small shows of selected artists for the gallery.

This was one of my most favorite things to do. Take a blank wall and with the artist's work, form it into something of beauty, something that made sense, that intrigued and invited curiosity, that was pleasing to the eye, and that showed off each piece to its best advantage. After doing this for a while, I proposed to the gallery owner that she could start a home service where we could take the art in someone's home and rearrange it to show off each piece to its advantage and then supplement one's collection with pieces from the gallery. Sharon jumped onto that idea and put me in charge of planning it and organizing it and basically working out all the intricacies and nuances that were required for it to succeed. But before I jumped into that, she had one last important show she wanted me to prepare: that for a photographer by the name of David Gillespie.

Nope. Never heard of him, but he had heard of me, not because I was famous, but rather because Sharon had told him that I would be handling the curation of his show, and David never left anything to chance. He had stalked me with this camera that night of the party, and unbeknownst to me, he had taken several hundred photos of me that night, studying my every movement. When he saw me struggling on the dance floor, he made his move. My talent wasn't enough for him. He needed me to be in love with him to ensure his show would be a success.

The first few weeks of our romance were a whirlwind. He pursued me relentlessly, and although I was embarrassed about the circumstances around which we had met, I felt flattered by the lavish attention. There were flowers, small gifts, large gifts, delicious meals, outrageous parties. David really worked it in the weeks leading up to his show. To me, it was exciting and new and fun.

And I had fallen hard.

DAVID GREW UP in a poor family with an alcoholic father who beat him and his brothers on a regular basis. Their mother was helpless against protecting them or herself, and David vowed in his young life that he would never again be poor and he would rescue his mother from this living hell. David earned a scholarship to the Vevey School of Photography. This happened when film turned toward the digital age and photography as he knew it was changing rapidly. David wanted to be at the forefront of this change, and he knew this would be the way he could save himself and his mother—to hell with his brothers. They could figure it out on their own.

While in his sophomore year of college, away in Jerusalem on an internship, David got word that his father had killed his mother in a rage of violence. David was devastated yet couldn't go back. He never returned for his mother's funeral, and he never came in contact with his family members again. Instead, he threw himself into his work and his studies, surpassing everyone in his classes and even the professors who taught him. He was devoted to his photography and used it as a vehicle to tell potent stories. That was one thing David and I had in common. We could take the things around us and turn them into an intriguing story that others could clearly see and understand.

By the time he arrived in Denver for his upcoming show, he had established himself in this field and was well respected despite his sometimes prickish nature. Because of his tumultuous childhood, David had an insatiable need for control—of everything and everyone around him.

Getting David into our gallery was quite a coup, but I wouldn't have been able to pick him out of a crowd—hence my not having a clue as to the identity of my mystery man when he rescued me the first night we met.

His show was a huge success; he received glowing reviews from all but one of the harshest critics. No matter what accolades he had received from respected colleagues and critics alike, none of it mattered to David except the one that stated he still had a long way to go.

A few weeks after the show, David asked me to marry him. It had only been a period of a few months that we had known each other, but I immediately gushed, "Yes."

It was one of the happiest times in my life. Here was a gorgeous man, a successful man, and he had chosen me. I finally felt like I had done something right, that I had finally become the woman I needed to be in order to earn his love. In that moment, I never could have known just how much that faulty thinking would cost me.

Evil and hate dwell within; jealousy and envy prevail. Betrayal and trickery overrule, where love appears to fail. A wicked serpent shall curse the land and leave his darkened mark. Salvation reveals one frail of flesh but with a mighty heart. The curse will turn these lands to black with dismal hue. Two kings shall pass; a queen shall reign and have to start anew. Courage and kindness are the mark of the Golden Creature to emerge. And from these lands, at last, the vile curse shall finally be purged.

~The Maasakai Kingdom Prophecy

THERE ONCE WAS A MAGICAL time when the Maasakai Kingdom was ruled by the animals. A peaceful dynasty of mighty and noble lions brought bounty to the land. This reign continued for centuries after humans came into existence; people lived and worked in harmony beside and with the beautiful beasts. It was the first humans who brought with them the Maasakai Prophecy.

Each and every member of the Maasakai Kingdom, before they could walk, knew the prophecy and how it came to pass. The story of the prophecy had repeatedly been handed down from one generation to the next and shared only on special occasions. It was the most beloved story of the children, who begged to hear it time and time again. Every individual had their own unique way of telling the story, but it was Enitan, the matriarch of the African bush elephants, who told it best of all.

One of the great heroes, pivotal in unfolding the events of the prophecy, was indeed an ancestor of Enitan.

According to legend, the story of the prophecy was told on each full moon. As her young daughter snuggled beside her, Enitan recounted this epic tale.

NOT SO LONG AGO, tragedy befell our peaceful kingdom. Such is the way when two young lions both fall in love with the same young lioness. The two young lions I speak about are Prince Numbalo and Prince Loki.

Other than their love for Princess Kazi, these two had absolutely nothing in common in either their looks, their demeanor, or what was in their souls. Where the children of the village would dance around Numbalo and squeal with delight as he passed out treats and small gifts, they would run to the opposite side of the path whenever Loki moved rapidly through the village with a deep scowl on his face and nothing but a sneer when someone would wish him good day.

Numbalo's smooth, dark fur glistened in the sunlight—sunlight that danced upon the muscles defining his strapping body, muscles assertively flexing and contracting with his every move. His proud, broad face displayed and expressed profound joy and made everyone in his presence glad to be there. With Loki around, it was plain awkward—the way he moved, slouched over, his eyes darting this way and that, never looking directly at you. Loki wouldn't smile, and the way he mumbled in that quiet voice of his discouraged conversation. The children were all very uncomfortable around him, and most adults were too.

And then there was Princess Kazi.

"You mean Queen Kazi?"

"My sweet. You are getting ahead of the story. For now, she is Princess Kazi."

Born to lead her people, the gifts blessed upon Princess Kazi made her truly extraordinary.

Princess Kazi was not aware of her powerful gifts and simply went through her days doing what came naturally to her. The children were drawn to her, for she always had a kind word and a quick smile to share with those around her. Because of her compassion and deep kindness, the power of her presence and being inspired others to live and be the same way. She lived a life dedicated to her growth of compassion and consciousness, and through this quiet dedication, she helped all those around her. Her kindness and generosity were always given freely. For her, it was effortless, an exquisite strength.

KAZI AND NUMBALO were destined to be together; everyone assumed so. Each day, they agreed to meet at the riverside, and Numbalo would bring Kazi a flower for her to wear in her hair. He placed it gently behind her ear as she gazed into his hickory colored eyes, revealing his love for her. She'd lift up onto her haunches and favor him with a kiss on his forehead.

"Eew, Mama, you can skip this part."

"Oh no, sweet girl. I must tell it all."

Some days, he brought her a Transvaal daisy, its thin, bright yellow petals that resembled an exploding firework. Other days, he gifted her a brilliant coral petal from a Watsonia flower or a periwinkle bloom from an African lily. But her favorite flower of all was the impala lily, as prolific in these lands as the impalas themselves. She loved the deceptively delicate-appearing five petals that made up the shape of a star, rimmed with a vivid pink border and a center to match. The star shape made her think of nighttime when, most often, she found herself resting by the riverbed, gazing at the stars.

"I love stargazing, Mama, just like Queen, I mean Princess, Kazi!"

"Yes, love, it is one of my favorite pastimes as well."

Receiving an impala lily made Kazi think of the night and the stars in the sky, which she watched with rapture for hours each evening, lost in thoughts—thoughts of her people, thoughts of her love for Numbalo and the beautiful life they would share and thoughts of her own purpose in life. She most often questioned her reason for being alive and what her contribution to the kingdom and legacy would be. The beauty of the stars, the beauty of the flowers, the beauty of the animals, and most of all the beauty of the people from her village fed her soul and bestowed upon her a prevailing sense of comfort and joy.

Loki also came to the river; only he would slink through the foliage and spy on Numbalo and Kazi. Consumed with jealousy and a burning rage that Kazi did not love him, he tortured himself day after day by watching their tender exchanges. This blinding rage and jealousy made Loki susceptible to Yolo's corruption and wickedness—Yolo, the malicious cobra who prowled the outskirts of the lands in search of life eternal.

"Mama, I don't like Yolo!"

"I know, my darling. None of us do."

Loki's jealousy made easy fodder for the evil serpent. If Numbalo became king, Yolo knew he would never be allowed to enter these lands. No promise could entice Numbalo to compromise himself or this kingdom for Yolo to get what his dark heart desired. Despite being known for his craftiness, Yolo knew Numbalo was wise to his wicked ways and would never yield to his trickery. Loki, on the other hand, was a different story. Yolo had witnessed from afar Loki's despair in the face of Kazi's love for Numbalo.

When it came time for Kazi to marry, a wrestling contest would be conducted to win her hand. Given the constitution of the two suitors, everyone took it for granted that Kazi would be married to Numbalo. Numbalo solemnly understood the seriousness of the contest; his training and dedication to excellence shored up his confidence in his ability to beat Loki. No one had any doubt as to the outcome, but the contest was the kingdom's tradition, and tradition always prevailed.

KAZI AND NUMBALO fell deeper in love, and one day, that exceptional love resulted in Kazi being gifted with a new life growing inside of her. Kazi knew the moment she had been blessed, but she held her happy secret silent and decided to reveal her joyful news the day Numbalo and she were married.

The week arrived of the wrestling contest with the wedding to follow the next day. Throughout Loki's entire life, he had been unfavorably compared to Numbalo, and it made him miserable.

"Oh, Loki, why can't you hunt like Numbalo? Loki, why can't you catch as many fish as Numbalo? Loki, why are you so slow to craft your tools? Loki, why can you not run as fast as Numbalo?"

On and on it went. As a result, Loki cultivated a deep hatred for Numbalo.

Under the cloak of darkness on the night of the new moon, Loki trained for the wrestling contest in a far-off field, so as not to be embarrassed by the prying eyes of the other villagers, when out of nowhere, Yolo appeared before him. Justifiably frightened by this arrival, Loki became most apprehensive when Yolo began to speak in a gravelly whisper so low and difficult to hear that Loki soon found himself face-to-face with Yolo, when just moments ago he had been a safe distance away.

"Loki, my friend, why do you sit here sulking in such darkness when both Kazi and the kingdom Numbalo will rule should be yours? Ah, ah, ah, don't say a word. Just listen."

Seductive words dripped from the cobra's mouth. "I can give you the power to seize the kingdom of Maasakai and snatch Kazi for your bride. I need but one teensy-weensy little favor from you. I need only for you to allow me back into the folds of Maasakai and allow me to roam the lands at night. No one will ever know I am there."

Loki had every reason to be leery and untrusting of Yolo, but so consumed by desperation and desire for Kazi, he saw no other way. Kazi was so alluring, so free, so full of life and light. He needed to possess her.

IT DIDN'T TAKE MUCH convincing or time for Loki to agree to Yolo's terms. What Yolo laid before Loki was akin to a treasure trove of gold and precious gems placed before a desperate and greedy man. He reluctantly agreed to allow Yolo to help him win the wrestling contest in exchange for granting Yolo permission to roam the lands at night. This triggered the prophecy, as Yolo cast his evil curse over the lands of the Maasakai.

"The young elephant repeated in time, along with her mother: Evil and hate dwell within; jealousy and envy prevail.

Betrayal and trickery overrule, where love appears to fail.

A wicked serpent shall curse the land and leave his darkened mark.

Salvation reveals one frail of flesh but with a mighty heart.

The curse will turn these lands to black with dismal hue.

Two kings shall pass; a queen shall reign and have to start anew.

Courage and kindness are the mark of the Golden Creature to emerge.

And from these lands, at last, the vile curse shall finally be purged."

KAZI AWOKE the morning of the contest full of nervous energy. She woke with the certainty that Numbalo would win her hand, for he had already won her heart. She was bursting to share the news of their child waiting to be born. Across her mind flitted the thought *Nothing is guaranteed,* and she shivered at that notion. Shoring herself up, she shook the feeling away and smiled at her foolishness.

Kazi reflected back to when she and her best friend, Ramla, would spend evenings at the river looking up at the stars. She remembered the story Ramla told her time and time again, pointing out the patterns of the planets and the stars and the fate they laid out for Kazi and Numbalo. Kazi couldn't see it, but Ramla could. She interpreted these patterns and assured Kazi that one day she and Numbalo would be husband and wife. Of course, Numbalo would win. They were fated to be together, for it had been written in the stars.

Kazi dressed in her finest cloak of red, for Numbalo loved to see her in red. He said it brought out the fire in her eyes and the flame of her desires, for which he loved her wholeheartedly. She then donned her delicately beaded white cap and collar. She looked splendid.

NUMBALO AWOKE feeling uneasy, yet choked down his meal and began to prepare. No one knows exactly how it arrived, although there are many rumors, all of them with Yolo behind the deed. A message arrived for Numbalo to meet Kazi at the river before the commencement of the competition. Although highly unusual, Numbalo rushed to the river to see his beloved. As he approached the river, his uneasiness returned. All was silent around him. More than this absence of sound was a complete void, not a bird to be heard, nor a whisper of a breeze in the trees. By the time the grave danger about to befall dawned on him, it was too late.

He froze in place as he noticed some rustling in the grasses surrounding him; his mind raced through thousands of possibilities in a single microsecond. In a flash, they were upon him, hundreds of snakes coiling around him, shredding his hide with their fangs.

He could hear Yolo's unmistakable voice in the background, urging them on, "Yes, my pretties. Feast upon his flesh so that you may live."

Numbalo fought mightily, attempting to fend off the attackers with his large and mighty paws. He roared with fury and pain, but to no avail. The snakes were too numerous and too vicious to be thwarted.

They ravaged Numbalo, leaving him for dead. He put up a steadfast effort, but no matter how valiantly he fought, the wounds were too numerous, and the blood flowed too swiftly for him to battle off his attackers. The relentless assault continued until the devils had their fill and finally abandoned their merciless attack.

Numbalo lay lifeless for hour upon hour until he awoke at dusk, that time of twilight when the light upon the earth seems almost dreamlike and ethereal. Twilight, the magical and mystical moment in time because it is liminal, neither here nor there. The space between, full of limitless potential and possibilities. The place in time when anything can happen.

"Ohhh, poor Numbalo."

"Poor Numbalo, indeed."

Numbalo could barely lift his massive head and found himself in excruciating pain. He felt as though every bone in his body were broken. His silken hide was in shreds, and he lay in a pool of his own blood, now crisp from the heat of the African sun and holding him to the ground like shackles. He knew it was dangerous to remain so vulnerable out in the open savannah. He ever so slowly dragged himself into the brush, far in the distance, and began licking his wounds.

THE VILLAGER'S FERVOR and desire for the upcoming betrothment was palpable, so convinced they were of Numbalo's impending victory. Families dressed in their finest clothes. They danced and sang songs of abundance, blessings, and praise on their way to the village center. Throughout the village, the contagious energy of the songs and the excitement and enthusiasm for the contest to take place grew and grew. Loki found himself the first to enter the center of the ring made up by the gathered villagers. He felt apprehensive. Although Yolo had assured him he would win the contest, and in turn, win Kazi as his bride, he was not privy to the details of how he would triumph. The crowd waited in respectful silence for Numbalo to take his place in the ring. When he did not appear, the silence turned to nervous restlessness as the villagers shifted their weight from side to side and tapped their walking sticks on the hard earth below them.

Numbalo's younger brothers were sent to his hut to find him. When they returned with worried expressions on their face and no sign of Numbalo, the crowd exploded in a chorus of yells, jeers, and questions.

"Where is Numbalo? Why isn't he here? What could possibly have kept him away?"

"Oh, Mama, I don't like this part."

"I know, dear one. I don't like it either."

In the entire history of the Maasakai, this had never happened before—a contestant failing to appear for the contest. The winner had to be delivered by day's end. The elders were perplexed, but at midnight, they declared Loki the winner by default, but the winner, nonetheless.

The villagers were angry at the decision that had been made and felt they had been cheated somehow. Kazi's heart broke wide open. Not only because she now had to marry Loki, but she dreaded the thought of what had happened to her Numbalo. She knew in the depth of her soul that something horrendous must have happened to him, for nothing would have kept him away.

Kazi wept tears of bitterness and grief throughout the night. She could not refuse the upcoming marriage. Despair filled her heart; what was supposed to be the most joyous time of her life had now become a time of great sorrow. She was strong and knew she could withstand just about anything, but she feared for the life of her unborn child. She did not know how she could possibly continue to keep her secret, but she would have to find a way until she could discover a solution to her predicament.

In her anguish, she thought sleep would never come, but at dawn, she felt her eyelids flutter open and her mind and body began to wake. Ramla remained by her side, helping her to prepare for the day. Both felines were fairly silent as the preparations began, and Ramla found herself comforting Kazi with a loving hug, a quiet caress, and the tender way she fixed Kazi's hair. The deep affection these friends had for one another was undeniable, and volumes were shared between the two women without a word passing between them.

As the two confidants began to proceed to the altar for the wedding, Ramla broke down and wailed, "Oh Kazi, this is so unfair. You belong with Numbalo. Everybody knows it. If I could, I would trade places and marry Loki myself so you wouldn't have to!"

"I know, my dear friend," Kazi softly replied, "but I must take my place in the kingdom, and Numbalo will always belong to me in here." She tapped her heart. *And in here,* she thought to herself as she unconsciously placed her hand atop her belly. She smiled at her best friend.

"It could be worse, you know. I'm not quite sure how, but things could be worse."

Ramla shook her head in amazement at Kazi's fortitude. Her friend had always been hopeful, expectant, and encouraging in the best of times and in the most trying of times, carrying along those around her.

"And this, my darling, was the most trying of times and about to get worse."

"Oh no, Mama." And she buried her head deeply into her mother's trunk.

The marriage took place with little fanfare based upon what is customary at a royal wedding. But the villagers did their best to offer up what little joy they could muster, so as not to offend their new king. Kazi was relieved when it was over, and Loki was disenchanted with the whole thing, as he realized that Kazi belonged to him in name only. He would never be able to capture her heart or her love as effortlessly as Numbalo had. Between them was an unspoken agreement. They both retired to separate chambers following the ceremony and festivities with barely a "good night" passing between them.

THAT EVENING, a feeling of uneasiness had settled upon Kazi, causing her to be considerably restless. She knew something was terribly wrong—something so grave and treacherous it fell beyond her comprehension. Sleep eventually overcame her, but when she awoke at dawn, her unease was affirmed. In a blink of an eye, her body told her everything she needed to know. Numbalo's disappearance, her marriage to Loki, the devastation that lay before her could only be the work of Yolo. The Maasakai Prophecy had come true. Terrified of what this meant for her people and all the animals that depended on this land for survival, she shook with anger. She raged at Loki for being so weak and allowing this to happen, and she was devastated at the loss of her beloved Numbalo—who should have been her king, her partner, her lover.

She raced into Loki's quarters and screamed at him, awakening the oblivious young man. "How could you?" she shrieked. "Look at what you have done. Our people and the animals shall surely perish. You fool. What exactly did Yolo promise you?"

Stunned, Loki rose from his bed to look out the window. The ruin before him brought him to his knees, and he wept silently. Dust fell upon the earth like rain. The villager's fields had disappeared overnight. The people's crops dried up and lay upon the land like brittle shells that simply disintegrated upon being touched. The livestock were nowhere to be found. The birds and the wild animals that normally wandered the grounds, the animals that Kazi loved so much, had vanished into thin air. The river they relied upon had rescinded to a trickle.

"Kazi, we must get away from here. Pick up only your necessities. We will leave within the hour."

Kazi hung her head, hating to leave the only home she had ever known. She had been so truly happy here and hated to walk away, but given the current circumstances, it was the only way to survive. Kazi and Loki led their tribe out of the village and headed north along the river. The remaining animals followed behind.

After enduring a long, tiresome journey, the gods eventually smiled upon them, for within a few days, they came upon an abandoned settlement and made it their own. The villagers could only hope they would be able to return to their homeland soon. Now that the villagers and animals were out of immediate danger, Kazi found her resolve beginning to dissolve. She was holding so much, grieving the murder of her lifelong love, concern for the safeguarding, preservation, and wellness of her people, the fate of the child developing within her, and most of all the uncertainty and fear that Yolo would discover their new location and they would forever have to be on the run to survive. It was too much for one woman to hold, but Loki was useless and had allowed the kingdom to fall into ruin.

Kazi had always been able to see the silver lining, but she had never been assaulted on so many fronts at once. It felt as though the sky were collapsing in on her at a relentless speed. She was determined to keep it together for the sake of her people and the child within her, but it was becoming more difficult with each passing day. Kazi had always taken great care of herself, but slowly, her daily rituals that kept her feeling so strong were slipping away. She was consumed in a downward spiral without recognizing the harm that was befalling her.

NUMBALO CONSIDERED himself lucky to have survived the brutal attack. He wasn't dead yet, but he would be soon if he remained alone without any help. He couldn't roar to summon aid, for that would alert his tormentors that he was still alive. He had to remain silent and hidden as he found a safe place to conceal himself and heal. Numbalo gingerly made his way through the brush and the forest speckled with the majestic acacia and jacaranda trees until he found himself a place by the old baobab tree.

"You know the funny one that looks like it's upside down?"

"You mean the one by the river?"

"Yes. That very one, my darling."

Frightened that first night, Numbalo didn't know if he would live or die. When he awoke, he found the unlikeliest of creatures bowed before him with a bowl full of fresh water.

"Why, Virgil. What are you doing here, my boy?"

Virgil, a young zebra, was tremendously brave, for Numbalo could have eaten this little guy for a snack, but Virgil stood before the prince, bowing deeply, and replied, "Your Majesty, I came to the river for a drink, and I stumbled upon you. I thought you were dead. I brought you some fresh water to drink."

"You are a good boy, Virgil. Thank you."

"I'm so glad you're alive. Something terrible has happened at Maasakai. Loki has claimed the throne of the king, and he means to harm us all. He's gone crazy. He's married to the princess—"

At this, Virgil stuttered, and his words came to a halt. "I mean—" and he deeply blushed as he hung his head, for the princess was to have been Numbalo's queen.

"It's all right, my boy. I understand. I need to know the truth. I need to know what's happening."

With this encouragement, Virgil started up again.

"Well, he's led everyone off the royal grounds and won't let anyone near him or the queen except for Yolo. No one knows if the queen is alive or—"

Virgil trailed off again, and this time, Numbalo was grateful the words had been left unsaid.

"Virgil, you have been very brave, and I am so happy that you have found me. Do you think you can help me?"

"Yes, your Majesty, anything. What can I do? Will it be like a secret mission? Will I be a spy or a double agent, or oh, how about a double-double agent?"

With his mounting excitement, his fear dissipated.

"Yes, my lad. A double-double agent it is! The first thing I need you to do is find Kazi, and if she is alive, give her the message that I am here. Tonight, I need you to bring the elders of Maasakai to me so we can figure out what is happening before it is too late. I will be here waiting."

So Virgil went off galloping toward the lands beyond Maasakai in order to find out if the queen was alive.

Virgil convinced the elders to follow him to the old baobab tree after dark. But he had no luck that first day finding the queen, or the next day, or the next, or the day after that. But on the fifth day, when he did find her, he almost didn't notice her. Kazi, low to the ground, had her back to him and was moving almost imperceptibly. When he did catch a glimpse of her, Virgil thought it was very strange that she should be in such a desolate place away from the new settlement.

Startled and angry when Virgil called out to her, the queen snapped, "Virgil, you should not be here. What do you think you are doing?"

"I can't believe I found you. I've brought you a message from the prince."

"I have no interest in what that heinous beast has to say. Leave at once!"

"Oh no, Your Majesty, you misunderstand me. I bring you a message from Prince Numbalo."

The queen was thoroughly confused and looked, well, she looked like how Virgil felt when he tried to keep a secret.

"Virgil, you naughty boy! It is wicked to tell lies. Numbalo is dead. Now away with you before I eat you."

Virgil no longer felt like a brave and heroic double-double agent, but he took a deep breath and continued on.

"My lady, I am sorry, but Prince Numbalo sent me here to find you and give you the message that he is alive but maybe not for long. He has already met with some of the elders."

The queen's head whipped around, and she stared hard at Virgil.

"You better not be telling lies, Virgil."

"It's true. I swear. He knighted me as a double-double agent and sent me on this mission."

Queen Kazi had to laugh. That did sound just like her Numbalo to indulge and delight the young ones and to feed their fantasies.

Kazi quivered with joy at the news Numbalo was alive, yet she continued her strange movements.

"Virgil, come here. I promise I won't eat you."

As Virgil approached the queen, she allowed him to pass, and he stammered, "My lady, why, there's one, two, three—three babies here."

"Yes," she laughed. "Yes, Virgil, there are three babies here. These are Numbalo's cubs, and I must get them away from here as quickly as possible. I have been gone from the settlement for far too long. Loki grows suspicious, but if he finds our babies, he will kill them. Can you come back tonight and take our boys to their father?"

"It will be my honor, Queen Kazi."

Our young hero returned that evening and took those cubs to the old baobab tree where Numbalo was waiting. You've never seen such surprise nor such joy when Numbalo first laid eyes on his sons. He licked them and cradled them in his magnificent paws as they all lay down to sleep.

The queen abandoned her hideout to return to the new settlement, to the evils that awaited her there. Her only solace was that the newborn cubs may have a fighting chance in the company of their father, her dear Numbalo.

LOKI WAS NOT GOOD to Queen Kazi even though they were now betrothed. He had always loved her, but he knew deep down she would never love him the way she loved Numbalo. Her continued kindness toward him, even though he had behaved so badly, only embarrassed him and made him feel so ashamed that he treated her worse and worse as time went on. He was humiliated by how easily Yolo had tricked him into putting everything and everyone in great peril. Kazi did nothing to provoke him, but her mere existence angered him. Kazi fell into a deep depression and gave up hope that anything could ever be good again.

She passed through the settlement with limbs heavy from despair, her heart beating with a sadness she could not shake. Her once stunning coat was now shockingly mangy and dull from days of neglect. Where she had been round and ripe with life, she could now feel each rib when she moved as her appetite had left her. Her visits and words of comfort had kept the other's hopes alive that this dark time would pass. Yet this time, she could see the light behind the villager's eyes had gone dim. She didn't blame them—the danger, the uncertainty, and the continuing devastation were enough to tear anyone down. The evil veil cast by Yolo continued to spread like wildfire. There were no signs of relief and no indication the Golden Creature even existed. Only Kazi and the elders understood that if the Golden Creature didn't come soon, all would be lost.

The people and the beasts of the land lived in paralyzing fear. The lands were dry, the earth scorched, food became difficult to find, and it was everyone for themselves. The dark and gloom of the curse were pervasive; they lived amidst the oppressive terror day after day. Kazi, too despondent to continue her rounds, did not pass through the settlement again.

Recalling the prophecy, the animals recounted:

"Evil and hate dwell within; jealousy and envy prevail.

Betrayal and trickery overrule, where love appears to fail.

A wicked serpent shall curse the land and leave his darkened mark.

Salvation reveals one frail of flesh but with a mighty heart.

The curse will turn these lands to black with dismal hue.

Two kings shall pass; a queen shall reign and have to start anew.

Courage and kindness are the mark of the Golden Creature to emerge.

And from these lands, at last, the vile curse shall finally be purged."

THE ANIMALS HAD FINALLY spotted the Golden Creature over the past several days. It traveled around in a great big truck surrounded by men with guns. Even though the animals were afraid, they crept from their hiding places in hopes of catching a glimpse of the Golden Creature. Every animal in the kingdom and the ones beyond knew the tale of their savior. And although each and every clan held out hope, no one really knew if the prophecy they had heard from one generation to the next were true. But here it was. The Golden Creature was come.

News such as this spread far and wide. The animals of Maasakai traveled across the lands in hopes of seeing the one who would save them and bring peace and abundance to their dangerous and desolate land. Day after day, the Golden Creature traveled with these men in the truck, and though they feared the guns, the animals continued to come forth from the shadows. Highly unusual for the animals to expose themselves by offering themselves up for the Golden Creature to feast its eyes upon so that it may see them and understand, understand they needed it—they needed its help, its strength, its courage. It was, indeed, the one they were waiting for.

TIME CONTINUED TO PASS, and although most of Numbalo's wounds were healing to some extent, his health was declining rapidly. Despite his agony, death would not provide relief until the Golden Creature had made itself known, and Yolo's wicked enchantment had been lifted. Night after night, our great Prince Numbalo met with the elders of the animal clans.

"Your great-great-great-grandmother was one of them."

"Nana Gigi was there!"

"Yes, my sweet, Nana Gigi was there."

They met in the cloak of darkness with the moon and the stars above as their only source of light. They knew they had to remove the Golden Creature from its station so that it could come and be amongst the animals, but they did not know how to get it away from the men with the guns. Time was growing short. If the Golden Creature did not come by the time the moon was full, all hope would be lost, and the entire kingdom would collapse. The days seemed interminable. The animals became more and more desperate and knew not what to do.

AS YOU CAN IMAGINE, Numbalo's rowdy pack of cubs was neither welcome nor desired at serious proceedings when their father met with the elders. But they were curious cubs, and after being fed and put to bed, they would silently creep from their resting place and hide among the rocks near where the elders gathered. The little cubs didn't know all the details, but they did understand they were all in grave danger, and just like any good lion does, they decided they were going to be heroes and come up with a plan to capture the Golden Creature. The cubs thought themselves quite courageous, and they were. They were very courageous and extremely clever.

The next day, they followed the stream of animals seeking the path of the Golden Creature. They bounded through the impossibly tall grass, chased after each other, and strayed every once in a while after a butterfly who captured their attention, swatting it from the sky with their oversized paws and missing the exquisite flying creatures more often than not.

The animals finally caught up to the giant truck and the men with guns. The little cubs stopped dead in their tracks and crippled themselves with laughter. This? This was the Golden Creature? This scrawny little girl who they could have captured more easily than the elusive butterflies they encountered? Without thinking, the cubs bounded forward into sight of the young girl. They tumbled and wrestled with each other. The cubs jumped and twirled in the air to capture her attention. They heard her exclaim at the sight of them, and soon the whole truck full was rumbling, exclaiming, and buzzing with excitement over the sight of the little cubs.

The cubs could hear and feel a furious deafening roar coming from behind them, and they knew they were in deep trouble. Numbalo had been diligent about keeping their existence a secret. They scampered out of sight and tried to avoid their father the entire way back to the rocks, but it was too late. The cubs had been seen.

THAT NIGHT, when the elders met, the chief of the Cheetah Clan spoke up and shared with the others the most extraordinary information. When the people of the truck heard the mighty roar, all of them trembled with fear and asked what would become of them.

All of them except the young girl who, he swore, exclaimed, "Oh, that's Numbalo. He is very angry with his children for coming out to play, but the animals need my help."

The elders all cheered, for this was the confirmation and the proof they had been waiting for. She was indeed the Golden Creature, and she had come to help them. They still needed to get her away from the men with guns. They discussed, debated, and argued all night long and still had no answer when the sun began to stretch across the sky illuminating and highlighting the landscape that next morning, but the cubs knew what to do. The following evening, while everyone was so busy arguing and talking, they were deep in action. The cubs knew they had to act fast and had to get to the girl while she was still enchanted by them. Numbalo's boys crept away from the elders and stole deep into the night, for they had to make it to the young girl's camp before sunrise.

THE GOLDEN CREATURE heard the lion that afternoon.

Knowing it was Numbalo and that his death was near,

she also recognized the danger at hand and the tragedy confronting the entire kingdom. The animals were calling her forth, her tiny body trembled with fear, yet she knew she must go. It was her destiny.

Hannah's new friend, Behatti, helped her with her plan. The girl did not intend to be gone for very long. Behatti told her where she could find the place Numbalo had secluded to and how she could get there without being seen. Because Behatti's mom worked in the kitchen, she secretly packed her a small bag with some food to take with her. Behatti told Hannah stories of the animals and what to beware of, but her broken English made it difficult for Hannah to understand what she said. They had made the plans, and Hannah wrestled with her decision. It was clear to her that this was a very stupid thing to do. She would most likely die. But she had been called forth and had prepared herself as best she could.

Hannah and Behatti agreed that it was time for Hannah to leave. The dear friends hugged one last time, and Hannah asked Behatti to watch over Dolly with instructions to take good care of her until Hannah returned. And if she never came back to keep her well forever.

AS THE CUBS ARRIVED at the camp, they checked to see where the Golden Creature was staying. They searched and searched until one of them spotted a doll laid in a chair on one of the front porches. Each one traveled 'round and 'round the hut a few times coming up with no further clues. Deciding they just had to take their chances, the cubs placed themselves below one of the open but shuttered windows and began to meow. Their caterwauling became increasingly louder until, finally, someone began moving around inside. The cubs hoped with all their might that the girl had awakened and not the men with guns. The girl inside the hut heard the cub's noisy calling and went to the window.

The shutters began to open very slowly with a great deal of trepidation.

"What does trepidation mean, Mama?"

"Well, my love, it means fear of the unknown."

It seemed like forever before the shutters opened enough for the cubs to see who was behind them.

The cubs heard a sharp snapping sound that could only come from an elephant and turned in alarm to see your Nana Gigi standing behind them.

160

"What are you doing here, you mischievous cubs? This is no place for you!" bellowed the matriarch as quietly as she could. Before they could protest, Nana Gigi's eyes grew wide. The cubs turned to see the young girl in the window. Her pale face was illuminated in the moonlight. Only this time, no laughter came forth regarding her appearance. This time they saw the Golden Creature and all her magnificence. Her radiant skin appeared as fine as a porcelain doll's as it shimmered in the moonlight. Her eyes were a deep aged cognac, yet if you looked at them long enough, you could see they were flecked with every color ever created in the heavens and sparkled in the starlight like the sun glistening off the river bed near their home. She was a pixie of a girl but more powerful here than when she was when flanked by the men with guns. Her fairy-like frame could not conceal the fierce spirit within her.

And her name was Hannah.

"That's my name, Mama! That's my name!"

"Yes, my sweet, that is, indeed, your name."

She rejoiced in seeing the cubs and somehow was not surprised. After taking each other in, the cubs continued the execution of their plan. Nana Gigi's anger dissipated as the cubs began frolicking below the girl's window, beckoning her out to play. The cubs knew the prophecy as well as any of them:

Evil and hate dwell within; jealousy and envy prevail.

Betrayal and trickery overrule, where love appears to fail.

A wicked serpent shall curse the land and leave his darkened mark.

Salvation reveals one frail of flesh but with a mighty heart.

The curse will turn these lands to black with dismal hue.

Two kings shall pass; a queen shall reign and have to start anew.

Courage and kindness are the mark of the Golden Creature to emerge.

And from these lands, at last, the vile curse shall finally be purged.

HANNAH'S DAD HAD LEFT very early for a project he'd been assigned to. Passed out from the celebration the night before, Hannah's mom lightly snored in her bedroom. She wouldn't hear Hannah leaving, although Hannah crept around quietly, as quiet as she could just in case. Hannah wanted to tell her mama so much about what she was about to do. She knew her mother would understand, but she would never allow it. So, Hannah must go without any discussion or explanation, without any goodbye.

It was dark when she left, but it was not pitch black, for the moon was waxing and shined its faint light upon the earth. Hannah had her little bag slung across her shoulder and chest, her miniature headlamp glowing brightly, and she eased her way out of the cottage.

She dared not kiss her mom as she walked out the door, but she whispered to her, "I love you so much, Mama. I'm sorry I didn't say goodbye."

And with that, the door swung closed behind her.

Nana Gigi's bewilderment turned to astonishment and then admiration as Hannah left her hut and joined the cubs. To Nana Gigi's amazement, Hannah was not frightened, not in the least. She petted the cubs and cuddled and kissed them, and then all five of them strolled through the camp and headed toward the cubs' home amongst the rocks.

As Hannah began walking through the camp, careful not to make any noise, she hoped she hadn't waited too long; she didn't want to encounter the staff making morning preparations. But for now, everything was quiet, and it seemed as though they were in the clear. She and the animals squeezed through the opening of the gate at the entrance to the camp. Hannah slipped through easily, for the gate was constructed to deter animals from coming in, not to deter humans from going out. They walked along the trails she had been driving on for nearly two weeks now, but she knew they must make their way into the brush soon before anyone came looking for her. They stepped into the high grass. Hannah felt badly about leaving her mom, but she knew at the same time that this was something she had to do, regardless of how dangerous and scared she may be. Hannah turned off her headlamp as the moon began to fade and the dawn gave way to a brilliant sunrise.

THE CUBS AND NANA GIGI had moved on ahead of Hannah. As she walked, she heard branches breaking that were not the branches under her feet. She stopped, and the sound stopped. She looked around but saw nothing. Hannah began once more—there it was again, the sound of branches breaking but not beneath her feet. She picked up speed, trying to catch the cubs, and the noise increased along with her. She came to the edge of a clearing, and though she knew she was supposed to stay hidden, she stepped out into the clearing to see if she could determine the source of this sound. Hannah felt a tap on her shoulder and nearly jumped out of her skin. She turned around, and right behind her was a baby elephant with his trunk extended to reach her. She reached out her arm in return, and he wrapped his trunk around it. They stood like this for a few minutes, just tangling and untangling their arms and trunk. He lifted his trunk and ruffled her hair. Hannah laughed aloud with pure joy as this little miracle paused by her side. When she moved back into the brush, he followed her. She turned around and saw him standing there, looking at her expectantly.

"Bye, little fellow. I am off to see Numbalo and to help rescue the kingdom."

The little one trumpeted with enthusiasm and trotted up to her side. They moved off, she and he. Pure magic and happiness flooded her body with this baby elephant by her side.

Hannah and Little Man had become instant companions.

Traversing the land soon became very tedious and tiring, yet Hannah and Little Man pressed on, carrying the unspoken urgency of Hannah's quest between them. Thirst overtook them, and they had to stop for a drink from the river nearby. Hannah was by the edge of the water. Little Man took a drink a short distance away. She saw a log float past and a really interesting stick; she took a few steps into the water to see if she could grab it. Without warning, the log lunged forward to grab her arm and pull her in. She fell over in sheer terror, and before she could comprehend the danger at hand, a huge hippo had emerged from underwater, forcing the crocodile back into the depths of the water. It took Hannah a short while to catch her breath.

At that moment, Hannah realized this was far more than a whimsical adventure, and for the first time, she comprehended the true danger before her and began to cry. Her tiny body was wracked with sobs as she pulled herself up the bank further from the edge of the water. Tired and scared and missing her mama terribly, she glanced around, ready to head home, when Little Man came to her side and helped her off the ground. He wiped her tears with his trunk and blew the hair out of her face. Wrapping his trunk around her shoulders, he nudged Hannah forward, and she and Little Man continued on their way.

IN THE CRUSHING HEAT, Hannah began to have serious doubts about the decision she had made. They came to a stream running no more than a trickle, but the gorge below was so deep that the timber traversing the expanse provided the only way to cross over to the other side. Where the cubs nimbly crossed the gorge at this very spot, Hannah and Little Man were extremely cautious. As they got to the end of the timber, it began to roll. Hannah tumbled off and fell to the ground. Hannah's leg got pinned between the log and a large boulder at the precipice of this gorge.

"Help!" she cried out. "Help!" she cried out again, wishing for the heavens to open and the hand of God to come down and save her from this trouble.

Little Man trumpeted loudly in distress. He stomped his feet, not yet strong enough to move the encumbrance off of her. He ran forth in search of Nana Gigi and the cubs. Surely, they could help.

Hannah could not move. She was overcome with devastating thoughts that she would undoubtedly die there either from thirst or hunger or be easy pickings for some ravenous animal. *What had she been thinking, coming here?* The sun now high in the sky beat down upon everything in its path, and her only saving grace at this point was the large acacia tree growing on the other side of the boulder. This tree provided life-saving shade for her poor stuck little body.

Hannah guessed it was midafternoon when Little Man returned with Gigi and the cubs. Gigi lumbered over and lifted the tree using her enormous trunk without much difficulty. Little Man had to encourage Hannah to crawl out from underneath it, which she finally did. Hannah pulled herself upright and hugged Gigi's huge leg in thanks. Gigi wrapped her trunk around Hannah's waist and hoisted her onto her back. It was terrifying and thrilling all at once. Hannah settled in and made herself as comfortable as she could, but she had never ridden an elephant before. With no further hesitation, our companionable little band of heroes headed off. To where, Hannah had no clue.

DELIGHTED WITH THIS NEW mode of transportation as they moved across the savanna, Hannah preferred this over trying to walk on her own. The captivating view from up high surpassed the view in the trucks that she had driven around in for the past couple of weeks.

She knew she should be afraid. She should be scared, but she was having far too much fun for that. Little Man and Nana Gigi stopped to eat some grass. Gigi put Hannah down, and Little Man nudged her forward and pushed the grass aside to reveal some of the largest, brightest colored berries Hannah had ever seen. She grabbed for one eagerly and scratched her arm on the spiny thorns as she withdrew her hand full of this magnificent fruit. She tasted it, and the juice dribbled down her chin. Hannah wiped it away with the back of her hand and then licked her hand clean. This was the most delicious fruit she had ever tasted in her short life. Gigi lifted her up again, and they were off. They continued across the plains at a lumbering pace, and Hannah suddenly felt not a care in the world.

As the sun began its final descent in the sky, Hannah and her companions arrived high in the rocks to meet Numbalo. Gigi gently lifted Hannah with her impressive trunk and placed her before Numbalo as carefully as a precious jewel. Numbalo studied Hannah for a long period of time. She had the good sense not to look him in the eye but rather averted her gaze down to see the lower portion of his stout body. Immediately, she saw the damage that had been done. She could tell his injuries were dreadful, witnessed by the blood and something oozing around his cuts as well. She didn't know if they were cuts, bites, scratches, or even from traps that she had heard the guide talking about. Hannah was pleased with her last-minute decision to take her mom's first aid kit and then wondered if Numbalo would let her get anywhere near him, much less allow her to tend to his wounded hide.

Gigi stood behind Hannah, Little Man behind her, and the cubs frolicked with excitement and pride at Numbalo's feet. Gigi had made up her mind that she would wait patiently until Numbalo decided to accept Hannah's presence. If Numbalo turned her away or worse, moved to attack, she would take Hannah back with her. They waited and waited while Numbalo paced back and forth, up and down, occasionally letting out a monstrous roar. He peeled back the flap of his lip over his frightful teeth, and his mouth opened as wide as a cavern. Hannah thought the roars were loud when she heard them from the trucks—they were deafening now up close amongst the rocks. The longer they waited, the more peevish Hannah felt.

You asked me to come, she thought to herself.

The dainty figure before him was not what Numbalo had expected.

It felt like a lifetime before Numbalo finally approached

Hannah and began sniffing her. She tried to stay relaxed so she wouldn't alarm him. But his whiskers tickled her skin, and she felt as if she would pee her pants. Every muscle in her little body had contracted and was stiff with fright. He took his muzzle and nudged and sniffed at the bag she had brought. Hannah slowly removed the bag from her shoulder and even more slowly opened it up and laid the contents of the bag on the ground before him. He continued his pacing, only this time around the contents of the bag. At least another hour passed before he approached Hannah again.

Then, he moved between Hannah and Gigi. This was it; he would either accept her or eat her alive. With his giant head, he gently rubbed Hannah up and down along the sides of her tiny body, welcoming her at last. With a mild roar, the three little cubs tumbled forth and begged her to come play. Gigi and Little Man took their leave. Little Man trumpeted his trunk one last time in a fond farewell.

Numbalo was in truly bad shape. He understood that Hannah had come to help, although he wouldn't let her get near his wounds. She tried to entice him with some of the treats from Akilah's kitchen, but he would have nothing of it. Hannah's body was spent and exhausted from the day's adventures, and she could barely keep her eyes open. Her place for the night was with the young cubs. The four of them flopped onto the ground in a tumbled heap, each of them struggling to find the most comfortable spot.

Days went by, and Numbalo still would not let Hannah near his lacerations. She was unclear as to what she should be doing other than waiting patiently. Hannah's feelings confused her, and she missed her mom terribly. She had made a really bad decision.

Or a bad choice, as her dad would say. "You made a very bad choice, Hannah." She could hear his voice in her head. "And now, you will have to pay the consequences."

Hannah couldn't even imagine what these consequences would look like—she didn't think even her dad could come up with an appropriate consequence for this.

HANNAH FELL INTO a loose routine as the days passed. Her favorite part of the day, by far, was going to the stream with the cubs and getting to see all the animals. The animals didn't come close enough for her to touch them— that seemed to be off-limits, but they behaved in a strange manner, similar to what she had seen when she came across the animals while riding on the trucks. The animals danced around and swooped their heads close to the ground, resting in that position for a few moments at a time—circling like dancers, gazing directly at her. Some of them brought berries left streamside for her to eat after they'd gone. What Hannah found most peculiar was although the adults wouldn't come near her, their babies were offered for her to touch, to caress, to nuzzle, to snuggle. The babies brought Hannah great comfort and cheer, and she continued to sing her sweet songs to all who came near.

HANNAH HAD A disturbing dream. She was surrounded by a tower of stones covered in ash, or it could have been a pit filled with snakes. She didn't know how she had come to be there. Although the snakes were aware of her presence, they didn't look at her. She found herself surprised that she didn't feel afraid in her dream but rationalized that she was aware she was having a dream and these snakes were not actually real. And if the snakes were real, there was no substance to them; they were almost transparent. When a snake did turn to look at her, it simply evaporated into thin air, and then the next, and the next—all evaporating into the air. There were two lions off to the side wearing the most extraordinary bejeweled crowns and capes she had ever seen, although the queen seemed agitated by Hannah's presence. Other scenes came into focus and then disappeared just as quickly, and Hannah could not make any sense of them. She saw a flash of the king drowning in the pile of snakes. She saw a grand parade of people and animals. She saw Numbalo lying lifeless upon a great rock that had significant meaning, but she was unsure of this meaning. When she woke the next morning, she knew that she must find this tower and the queen within it. She had clarity now. This is what they had called her for; this was her divine path.

NUMBALO LOOKED WORSE than ever. Hannah moved slowly over to him on her hands and knees, dragging her little bag with her. She began to tell Numbalo of her dream the night before and how she must find this tower of stones. She left out the part of his death, for she was not entirely sure. She could interpret his agreement because he let her take his paw and tend to his wounds without any dissent or argument. Hannah cradled his head in her lap as she inspected his wounds. She didn't know anything about medicine, but she knew the severity because the lesions smelled awful, so awful that Hannah thought she might throw up. But Numbalo, this royal creature, had accepted her presence, which meant it was up to her to help him. So she kept her gagging to herself and began to do what she could to help him. She used a little cloth that she moistened in a tiny nearby pool. Hannah wiped away the blood and ooze as best she could, but there was so much of it, and it kept coming. She had to scrub briskly in order to get close to the actual wounds. Numbalo kept lowering his head and pushing her hand away, but she persisted, hoping he wouldn't bite her.

Hannah started to cry. She was overcome with sadness, loneliness, and feeling so mixed up. She had a hard time cleaning and dressing Numbalo's wounds through her tears. And though Numbalo and Hannah both understood this was merely a temporary solution and would never fix him, he appreciated the gesture and licked her tears away with abandon. Again, his whiskers tickled her skin, and she giggled and squirmed around. The cubs were curious about the noises coming from her and pounced over to them. They jumped on their dad, who was purring in the way of a cat and continued to tickle Hannah with his whiskers, now intentionally instead of inadvertently. They all frolicked this way for a great deal of time, all of them thankful for a respite from the treacherous events ahead.

This was Hannah's last night to be with the cubs, and as they lay down to sleep, she hugged each one of them close to her body, wanting to remember every little thing about this moment and her time in the rocks: the way their fur looked so velvety and soft and yet felt almost as rough as a brillo pad; they were grey in color, not yet having developed their beautiful tawny coat and had even darker grey spots and stripes; their little ears looked like those of a teddy bear; and their sweet little faces looked like the face of her friend's kitty cat back home, not at all like the fierce lions they would become. Their growing claws were sharp and would occasionally catch on her clothes or her skin, leaving a mark, but she didn't care. Hannah just never wanted to leave. She had done all she could for Numbalo, and Hannah had but one task left. Hannah was a gift to the Maasakai Kingdom and a gift to Numbalo, providing comfort while this exalted king bided his time. She moved closer to Numbalo, taking his damaged paw into her petite hands. She began to sing every song she had ever known. It sounds crazy, but she really thought he enjoyed the songs from the *Lion King* best of all.

"I love the Lion King, Mama."

"I know you do, sweetheart; we all do."

She sang him the lullabies that her mother had sung to her when she was young and still did from time to time when Hannah wasn't feeling well. She sang to him the silly songs she had learned at camp and at school. And she sang to him every song she could remember from every musical she had ever seen. Hannah told him stories about growing up and what she liked about her family and the things she didn't like. Every now and then, he would lick her face or nudge her arm in agreement or approval. She sang late into the night. She sang until her throat was parched and her eyes snapped shut. When she awoke a few hours later, long before the sun had come up, she had to go pee. Numbalo licked her face as she got up to go. Hannah petted him on his splendid mane and bent over to kiss him.

"I love you," she whispered. "Thank you!" He nodded his head and licked her once more.

When she returned, Hannah curled up between his legs and cried herself back to sleep. Daybreak came far too early the next morning.

HANNAH AND THE LIONS moved out of the rocks and headed to the big river. Numbalo, at least for the moment, could come and get a drink on his own. Hannah sat by the water's edge and marveled at the world and the life that surrounded her. She was amazed at how very different the landscape and the makeup of the country were here compared to her home in the States. Behatti tried to describe to her, tried to tell her, but the words were unclear, and Hannah couldn't quite grasp her meaning. Now she understood even if they spoke the same language, she would never have been able to put into words the true makeup of this land. It was rough and magical, but the vast contrast of the rough to the splendor made her appreciate the wonder and magic all the more. She hoped she would make it back to tell Behatti of all she had seen.

It was time to leave Numbalo behind; his difficulty getting to the river indicated he did not have enough strength to make the journey to the tower with her. The elders assembled to help escort Hannah to find the tower of stones she had described from her dreams. They moved off from the river. Hannah promised Numbalo that she would return Kazi to him. He, in return, warned her of the dangers she might face.

Only Numbalo comprehended what else they would find there as he thought of the prophecy.

Evil and hate dwell within; jealousy and envy prevail.

Betrayal and trickery overrule, where love appears to fail.

A wicked serpent shall curse the land and leave his darkened mark.

Salvation reveals one frail of flesh but with a mighty heart.

The curse will turn these lands to black with dismal hue.

Two kings shall pass; a queen shall reign and have to start anew.

Courage and kindness are the mark of the Golden Creature to emerge.

And from these lands, at last, the vile curse shall finally be purged.

REUNITED WITH NANA GIGI as her guide, the two friends eased into a comfortable rhythm as they had before. At night, the elders gathered around Hannah, providing her with food, companionship, comfort, and safety. She loved sitting by the blaze of the evening fire intently listening to the stories that had been handed down generation from generation. The elders received delight in her keen interest and curious nature. They took turns telling her of the Maasakai Prophecy and what it meant for their people and the animals. She shared by singing her sweet songs of love and hope. Hannah loved these animals and their people. Animals had always brought her great comfort and joy; nothing pleased her more. She often fell asleep cradled in Nana Gigi's trunk, which rocked to and fro just as a baby cradle would. Hannah was wise beyond her years, yet in so many ways, she was sheer innocence. It was this pure innocence that marked her as the Golden Creature, and it was this pure innocence that would save the kingdom if she were able to defeat Yolo.

HANNAH'S LIMBS had grown sluggish and fatigued. She wondered if they would ever find the tower of rocks. Her resolve was weakening.

Who am I to save this magnificent kingdom and its people? This had become her new mantra, and it wearied her.

The uncertainty was driving her crazy and making her extremely restless.

Several nights into the journey, the elders all gathered and told Hannah they had spotted the tower that very day—they were close and would reach it tomorrow.

How did I miss it? she wondered.

Everyone agreed that Hannah's first task was to locate Kazi without being detected. The scouts who had gone ahead to do reconnaissance reported that the grounds and the tower were being guarded by snakes but confirmed what Hannah had witnessed in her dream: if she looked right at them, they would vanish into thin air, and she would be unharmed. Her little heart began to beat rapidly, and sweat broke out across her brow. She shivered despite the heat from the fire and the heavy blankets wrapped around her. Nana Gigi comforted her, reassured her, and once again rocked her to sleep.

Just before daybreak when they awoke, Hannah exchanged her final goodbyes with Little Man and Gigi, her forever friends who had been her companions and protectors.

KAZI HATED HERSELF for being so weak, but the responsibility was too much to bear, and the weight of the darkness too much for her to endure on her own. She saw no way out of this treachery and knew her people depended on her to save them from this devastation. Trapped within the darkness of the dwelling and overcome with hopelessness, the queen hid herself away, isolated from all of those she had once laughed with, lived with, cried with, and whom she at one point deeply trusted and loved. She felt unworthy of their love. Now she felt undeserving of happiness or joy. The darkness held her tightly in its grip and showed no signs of letting go. The queen had become unrecognizable, even to herself. She willed the world to stop spinning and wanted to just lie down and die. Her children were gone, and as long as Loki remained in power, she could find no reason to go on.

Her silent and slow descent caught her off guard. Try as she may, she just couldn't summon the strength or the energy to go and see the villagers. Tears fell as she considered all that had been lost to them. The children of the tribe must be frightened and confused, the grownups desperate for news of what was to come. Their world had been ripped out from beneath them and toppled upside down. Kazi resolved to attempt to console them—tomorrow. She was far too weary and too distraught to show herself now.

HANNAH WAS SURPRISED at how easily she entered the new royal grounds. She readily made her way across the rocks and the barren ground to the tower that lay before her. She knew Kazi must be hidden away in there, but she had no idea what she would find and no clue as to how Queen Kazi would react upon her arrival.

"Hannah was so brave, Mama, wasn't she?"

"She sure was!"

It took Hannah several attempts to find the location where Kazi had been concealed. Hannah gasped in alarm at what she found before her. Kazi lay on the floor in tatters, her eyes open just a slit, her eyelids puffy and irritated from the sobbing that had transpired for days on end. Kazi's body appeared so limp and lifeless, Hannah wasn't even sure she would have the strength to get up.

Her usual glistening, supple copper-colored fur was now

dull and ashy. Her clothes were in shreds, and she seemed to be slightly out of her mind the way she mumbled, moaned, and motioned urgently toward something Hannah could not see. Coursing through her body, Hannah's adrenaline caused her breath to come in short, yet powerful, bursts. Hannah felt as though every nerve of her being was electrified. She couldn't think. She couldn't feel, knowing that it wasn't just Kazi's life at stake but rather the whole kingdom and its beautiful beasts.

She saw a vision of Numbalo pulling her to Kazi's side and found herself kneeling alongside her, pleading for Kazi to look at her. Kazi was inconsolable, crying in Hannah's arms, begging to die between bouts of mumbling incoherently. Although quite upset by it all, Hannah was determined to do anything she could to aid the queen. Hannah took a deep breath and began singing, all the while holding Kazi in her arms and stroking her matted hair. Once Kazi finally calmed enough and quieted down, Hannah told her of her dream and why she had come to find her.

"We must get you well, and you must return to Numbalo for the curse to be broken."

"My child, you are sweet and kind, but I cannot go anywhere. Loki has me captive, and Yolo and his forces roam the grounds all hours of the day and night."

"Queen Kazi, forgive me, but no matter what evil forces are at work—somehow, we will come up with a plan." In a low whisper, she confided, "I know the secret of the snakes; it came to me in my dream."

Kazi shuddered with this knowledge, this revelation, that before her kneeled the Golden Creature—the one whose purity and innocence would set them all free. Kazi's heart brimmed with hope; she could not quite believe the Golden Creature had actually come.

So it went, day after day. Hannah would meet with Queen Kazi. Tenderly, Hannah cared for and tended to Kazi, who had become paralyzed by the fear and uncertainty of the dire circumstances before her. Hannah spoke of the deep affection, admiration, and devotion Kazi's tribe had for her. She spoke of hope and the brighter days ahead for Kazi, her people, and the animals. She asked Kazi questions that forced her to search deeply inside herself for the wisdom the child claimed she'd find within.

In the hours they were together, Kazi felt great comfort, grace, and even peace. Kazi's physical and spiritual health flourished under the Golden Creature's care. A hunger had been ignited within her, her ailing spirit and despondent manner were falling away, and an astonishing longing whispered to her in the night, which in turn, propelled her through the day—a longing to be reunited with Numbalo and her boys and restore her kingdom to its former magnificence, no matter what difficulties and hardships lay ahead.

THE TIME HAD COME; Kazi shared her plan with Hannah. She must not allow herself to succumb to the fear that Yolo had instilled in her and her people. It was time to be strong and defend her kingdom fiercely, to hold her head high and conduct herself with dignity. It was time for her to show her authority and lead with her loving heart. Kazi would align herself with Loki; it would take both of them to defeat Yolo. She would continue to appear as if weak and disoriented, for Yolo had no knowledge of Hannah's presence. She would look to Loki to flatter Yolo, to play to his vanity and arrogance and consuming desire for power. Surely, Yolo saw Kazi as no threat. They would have Loki summon Yolo to Kazi's chamber, pleading for him to save Loki's queen, to spare her life. Loki would promise anything and everything Yolo demanded. When Yolo drew near to her, Kazi would lash out and cut off his head. Once Yolo was vanquished, all could begin the journey to their homeland.

As requested, Hannah secretly addressed the villagers with the information given to her by Queen Kazi.

"Your queen has instructed me to relay this message," Hannah spoke, clearing her throat and speaking with great assurance. "Prepare yourselves for your return to the kingdom. A great celebration is close at hand; you will know when it is time to depart."

Hannah's ebullience was contagious—excitement, disbelief, and anticipation overcame the crowd that had gathered. This celebration would be unlike any prior. The crowd dispersed and immediately began their preparations as directed.

Kazi knew her plan was improbable, if not impossible, yet she had come to realize that the Golden Creature had been a precious gift sent to facilitate her own reclamation and healing. It was essential for Kazi to lay claim to the truth of her strengths that would help her tackle the great task ahead, that she alone was capable of. She had been ravaged both inside and out, dismantled beyond recognition, and like a phoenix rising from the ashes of all it once held dear, she, too, trusted that she and her people would rise into greatness beyond anything Kazi could imagine.

Kazi understood the words of the Golden Creature were meant for her. She saw her own gifts. She was love, compassion, joy, and healing; simply being in her presence touched the villager's souls. Her people experienced love, displayed compassion for one another, were joyful in their daily lives, and were healed by her presence.

Kazi would no longer accept the finality of her circumstances; she would rise and save her people and the beautiful beasts throughout the land. The moment had arrived, and Kazi readily accepted and acknowledged all of the magnificence bestowed upon her by the grace of God.

Kazi began her own preparations to lead her tribe to safety. Brief flashes of doubt and insecurity would creep in as Kazi focused on her plan, yet her resolve was so deeply anchored, she could not be dissuaded from freeing her kingdom of the curse.

KAZI WENT TO SEEK OUT Loki to tell him of her plan. She made her way through the once abandoned fortress now occupied by Loki, his officers, and the attendants. She found herself in the main chamber of the fortress, the walls of stone covered in lichen of varying hues of green, from the softest tint of celery to the warmest shade of pine. Its effect displayed a rich tapestry of color upon the aged walls. Kazi came alive to the wonder of the beauty that surrounded her, which was in deep opposition to the horror happening around her.

The damp and unfriendly surface beneath her caused a chill to run up and down her spine. She spotted Loki in the far corner of the room, unbelievably in conversation with Yolo, the vile serpent. Loki's shoulders were hunched over, the muscles in his body taut with fear. Kazi could see his eyebrows in a half-arch and his mouth open a fraction, which turned into a full gape when Yolo interrupted him.

"Well hello, your highness," Yolo began, his words drenched with sarcasm. "You got here just in time. I've been discussing the future of the kingdom with your husband here, and you especially may be interested to hear what I've come up with."

Yolo began slithering about, tormenting Kazi. Kazi looked around the chamber yet again, as her vision cleared, she could see hundreds of snakes creeping along the base of the walls; they had appeared out of nowhere. Hannah had not yet divulged the secret of the snakes. None of this was going as she planned; Kazi became crippled with fear.

Kazi wanted to speak to Loki in private to tell him the Golden Creature had arrived, but she could not make

Hannah's presence known to Yolo, for it would put Hannah in grave danger. She needed Loki on her side, and it was imperative that she adjust her original plan immediately.

With a forced smile, Kazi coaxed, "Loki, my king, please come to me. I am not feeling well, and I need your help. I do not know how much more of this I can take."

Oh, how long Loki had waited to hear those words from her. He was not foolish enough to mistake these words for love, but Kazi had sought him out, and that would have to do for now. Maybe someday she would come to love him, even if it were just a little bit.

Loki crossed the room to his bride's side. When she reached for his hand, he attempted to shield her from Yolo.

"Stop it. Stop it right now, Yolo!" roared Loki, "Leave here at once!"

"Leave! But why would I leave when the fun is just beginning? Loki, were you aware that your new bride is the proud mama of three young boys—three young boys who will one day come and exact their revenge upon you?"

Stunned by this news, Loki stammered as he began to respond. He looked to Kazi for denial, but none was forthcoming. Loki crumbled at the news; Kazi would never be his, and he became aware that in his desperation to possess her, he had destroyed his home and the lives of thousands.

All this pointless destruction launched from his own selfish hunger. He dropped to his knees, begging Kazi for forgiveness through his tears.

"I never meant to harm anyone," he said softly. "I never meant for it to go this far. Kazi, I have loved you since we were small. I so desperately wanted you to love me back, to know me, to even acknowledge me. I am so terribly, terribly sorry."

"I can tell you are, Loki," Kazi replied as she lifted her trembling hand to his face, this time with genuine affection. She spoke ever so quietly. "Listen to me. The Golden Creature has arrived. It is time for us all to return home, and our people have been preparing for days."

Shocked, Loki doubted, "Are you sure? Where did the creature come from? How long has it been here? How do you know it's real?" The questions continued to tumble forth.

"It's her, all right," Kazi answered. "But we need to act quickly. I did not realize that Yolo was here within the fortress."

"Is it true what Yolo said about the boys?"

"It is Loki, but you need not fear them. They will never attempt to avenge their father, for the Golden Creature brought happy news as well. Numbalo is not dead, as we all believed. He is alive and caring for our boys."

"Oh my god, Kazi. What have I done?"

"None of that matters now, Loki. What matters is getting our people back to our homeland, back to safety."

Their tender exchange was halted by the arrival of the Golden Creature, the appearance of Hannah.

The royal couple and Yolo all looked to her in surprise as she entered the chamber.

"That's quite enough, Yolo," Hannah insisted. "Loki is right. It's time for you to take your leave."

"I beg your pardon, miss, but I beg to differ." Yolo glided closer to where Hannah stood. He swayed back and forth but kept his head dipped, careful not to make eye contact with the Golden Creature. Yolo was the only one privy to the knowledge that if he were to make eye contact with the Golden Creature, she would die—but so would he.

Hannah and Yolo continued their assessment of one another, while Kazi and Loki crept closer to them from the opposite side of the vast chamber.

The air had become still with the exception of the eerie echoes of the reptiles moving along the walls.

Hannah cast a divine golden light all around her. Her light revealed the divine truth, and it was this truth that Yolo was afraid of, for he could not exist in its presence, and it was this he sought to destroy.

Hannah, remembering her dream and the evaporating

snakes, started to sing with a tremor in her voice. As her voice gained strength, she grew brighter and brighter. She appeared to be lit up throughout, as though being consumed by flames burning inside her. Kazi and Loki resisted looking away, even though the intensity of the blaze dared them to do so. Her angelic voice mesmerized all who were present, and they continued on in their silence. Hannah persisted with her singing. She willed Yolo to look directly at her, to meet her gaze, to look directly into her light. And he did.

As he lifted his head to strike her, Loki growled "Nooooo!" and leaped into the air. In the same moment that he lashed out to cut off Yolo's head, he was struck and poisoned by Yolo's venom.

Loki dropped dead to the hard earth. Yolo evaporated into nothingness, and Hannah was consumed by the flames from within. When the smoke from the smoldering embers had cleared, Hannah had vanished, and in her place was a patch piled high with glittering gems, beautiful just like the child.

Kazi wept heartfelt tears, for both Hannah and for Loki—tears for Loki who, in a most selfless act of heroism, had sacrificed his life so that the Golden Creature could live and fulfill the prophecy and tears for Hannah, who was lost to her as well.

Kazi would not linger; she had to get her tribe to safety and lead them back to their homeland.

She could hear the words of the Golden Creature from inside her head, the words the Golden Creature had spoken for days.

It is time for you to rise and lead your tribe back to your rightful kingdom. The villagers are ready, and Numbalo will be waiting for you.

Kazi was apprehensive about the enormity of the task before her, but she could still feel the child's presence as it urged her on. Kazi realized the true gift the Golden Creature had brought her was not the reclamation of the kingdom but rather the reclamation of herself. The child, in her magnificence, reflected Kazi's own magnificence back to her. Her pure radiance, love, and strength had reawakened Kazi's hope and desire to be the queen Hannah believed her to be. She now had the faith that she would find her way. The Golden Creature had shined a light onto the truth: Kazi's truth and the truth for her tribe. She finally saw what the child had seen; she saw her own divine courage, wisdom, and beauty. They had been with her all along. Kazi wept with gratitude before picking herself off the floor to attend to her tribe.

AND SO IT CAME TO BE that Queen Kazi led her people back to their homeland, back to her true love and her precious boys.

The villagers were ready to celebrate; there had been far too much darkness for far too long. Happiness and joy were long overdue. Although they had no way of knowing what awaited them, they had hope in their hearts, for the villainous Yolo had been defeated at last.

Several of Kazi's top spearmen were sent ahead to the homeland with a great number of the tribe joining them. They were to alert Numbalo of Kazi's pending homecoming and prepare the village as best they could.

NUMBALO HEARD IT FIRST, a low rumbling that grew into a steady beat he felt pulsating through the earth beneath his feet. His heart began to race. Kazi was near, his cherished Kazi coming home at last.

News spread quickly through the kingdom as Numbalo

gathered their boys. Everyone rushed to the village center to await the arrival of their queen. Most had not seen her since they had deserted the kingdom in what felt like a lifetime ago. The excitement in the air was electric as old friends and neighbors reunited and inquired after one another. Children ran about and buzzed with eagerness, not truly knowing what was at hand.

The drums continued to beat, all the while growing louder and more fervent with each approaching step. The anticipation of the crowd rose right along with the beat of the drums.

As Kazi's procession reached the hill crest just outside of the kingdom, the tusk trumpets were blown to announce her homecoming. The villagers at once recognized the unique sound of this royal side-blown trumpet and erupted into loud cheers. They soon quieted down in a respectful stillness, waiting for their queen to appear.

The pageantry began. A line of twelve soldiers straddled upon a dozen ostrich, each blasting the coveted ivory trumpets in unison to announce the queen's return. The ostrich, decorated in the finest silk of the deepest, most electrifying purple hue strode through the gates, setting the tone of the celebration. Line after line of soldiers and ostriches kept striding through the gates in waves. Next, golden chariots pulled by zebras and, occupied by Kazi's close infantry, crisscrossed through the village center. The men wearing splendid ruby silk robes were waving the flag of the kingdom high in the air as they bounced along the grounds. Across the plaza, women archers in bright blue—some lowered on one knee while others stood—raised their bows and arrows to the heavens and shot projectiles of ribbons into the sky, which unfurled with the grace of a blue crane as they cascaded to the earth, causing the audience at hand to gasp.

Women dressed in vivid red costumes with luminous beading and silk swung giant plumes of feathers as they made their way through the village dancing and twirling through the air. Hunters in their animal skins marched forward, tapping their javelins and enormous hide-covered shields in time to the drumbeats. The stockmen appeared amidst colorful powder in the air while waving flaming balls of hot iron. All the while, the drumbeat remained in the background. Hundreds of birds were released into the air, and the gathered crowd went crazy with excitement.

Attendants marked with white paint marched forward on stilts with empty gourds and platters atop their heads. As they entered the kingdom, the gourds filled with water and wine, the platters magically crowded with a huge variety of delectable fruits. The body of people became drunk on the delicious aromas in the air.

A hush fell over the crowd as thirteen men came forward carrying a palanquin. Upon it sat Queen Kazi, flanked on either side by an attending lion. Adorned from head to toe in colors that God must have created only for her, Kazi was resplendent in her lively royal cloak. But even those luminescent hues could not detract from her magnificence. Her eyes blazed like the finest gems when they first caught sight of Numbalo and her boys. The villagers began chanting, jumping up and down in place as Queen Kazi roared triumphantly as she rode through the crowd. Here was the Kazi they remembered, finally returned to them, quite possibly even more majestic than before, and the villagers fell in love with her all over again. The men gently rested the palanquin upon the ground, and Queen Kazi was presented to Numbalo. Kazi rose from her throne and stepped forward; her escorts fell in behind her. Kazi rushed to Numbalo's arms, and the couple was at long last reunited. She gathered her boys into her arms and breathed a huge sigh of relief. She smothered them with kisses, pulling them ever closer. Numbalo tapped her on her shoulder and pointed.

The rest of the beautiful beasts had returned, the splendid wild animals that had roamed and called these lands their home long before the Maasakai people arrived. The villagers wept at the sight of them. The magnitude of their return was staggering, and as the beautiful beasts came forward, a light rain started to fall. This rain began to heal the earth; the surrounding trees and brush burst forth with astonishing greenery. The fields, once dry and barren, now were dotted with foliage from the crops the villagers had thought were lost to them, and they soon heard the rushing of the river as it came to life at the edge of the kingdom. Villagers and royalty alike rejoiced at this unexpected chain of events. The curse had been lifted, the prophecy fulfilled. The Golden Creature had come, and the kingdom had been spared, but it was now up to Kazi to restore it to its former glory. In that jubilant moment, only Numbalo and Kazi remembered the line from the prophecy: *Two kings shall pass—*

THE MIST HAD DISSIPATED at last. Kazi and Numbalo were united as king and queen. Their union, the marriage they were destined for since the beginning of time, had come to fruition. At the conclusion of the abbreviated wedding ceremony, the villagers and processional made their way to the river to allow all, both the people and the beasts of the kingdom, to pay a silent tribute to their savior, the Golden Creature.

For the prophecy to conclude, a second king must pass. Numbalo had fulfilled his part of the prophecy by marrying Kazi, knowing full well that by doing so, he had written his own death certificate, for he was the second king. He had loved this kingdom and all its beings since he was a young boy, being groomed to care for its inhabitants since the day he was born. Now to prove that love, he willingly was ready to give his life, just as Loki had unselfishly given his so that Kazi could reclaim the kingdom as her own and save all those who resided within its borders.

Although Numbalo regretted that he would not be able to raise his young boys and instill in them the values that had been instilled within him, he was ready to succumb to death. They had all been through so much, he actually welcomed it like an old friend, knowing that Kazi was at the helm.

It was time for Numbalo to say goodbye to his wife and children and entrust the kingdom to Kazi's strong and benevolent hands—Kazi, the lioness of love.

Numbalo called Kazi forth with a toss of his head, and she sat beside him. She buried her face into his fur, gripping his mane as tightly as she could, and began to sob. Kazi didn't want to lose her beloved now. But her tears were futile. Twilight had settled upon the earth, and Kazi understood as much as Numbalo did that his death was imperative if any of them were to survive. The prophecy had to be completed. She alone would have to find the strength to rebuild the kingdom and go on without him by her side. She called their boys over and had them sit near their father. Kazi reflected on how monumental this moment was and wondered if the cubs would even remember it once they were grown. The beautiful beasts of the kingdom gathered 'round, and as each called out to their king, he silently, and without struggle, slipped away into the ethers.

HANNAH WALKED to her family's cottage, but no one was there. She could see her mother's things, but her mom was nowhere to be found. She went to find Behatti. As Hannah rounded the corner to the back porch of the kitchen, she spotted her mom through the screen door.

THE NIGHTS WERE the worst of all. At least during the day, for now, I had a little work at the gift shop each day. I met so many interesting people from all around the world who visited the camp and wandered through the shop to see if there was anything they couldn't live without. Conversations flowed freely unless they had heard the news of my daughter and realized who I was. The instant that happened, people clammed up, the conversations came to a halt, and they quickly left the gift shop. At night, the pain came. It felt as if my grief would never stop. Akilah often came in the night to check on me, just like I was one of her own. Her sisters and colleagues warned her not to befriend me. They insisted I would bring her nothing but trouble, nothing but bad things could come by my being here. I was an omen and a bad one at that. I would poison their community.

"She will poison us all with her bad luck—a child disappearing, a husband who leaves her behind—this is all bad luck and bad signs of what's to come if we keep her around."

Much to my advantage and delight, Akilah didn't listen to these warnings, and she chose to continue to be my friend, my caretaker, my cheerleader. Despite the awkwardness when people knew what had happened to me, the gift shop thrived. We had such a great business that we were able to bring in more goods and crafts from additional tribes and families in the area. It paled in comparison to American standards, but by the standards here, we were doing well and offering opportunities to families who previously had none. I felt good about that and took great pleasure and pride in the work I was doing at the shop. The others had no idea what I experienced at night. The voices in my head tormented me for being such a failure, for putting our daughter at risk in such an unfamiliar place where we didn't understand the language and we certainly didn't understand the culture. That I had offered up my little girl because I wasn't strong enough to handle life without a drink will haunt me until the day I die. It suddenly occurred to me that I hadn't had a drink since the night I confronted David and ended our marriage.

Ha, I laughed out loud, I hadn't even noticed.

Even the driving pain at night didn't turn me to drink for solace. I would survive this. I would survive without a daughter, without a husband. I would survive myself. I would simply survive just being myself. I let out a little whoop in celebration of this revelation. I felt clearer than I had in years.

I heard the roar of the lion again, the first time I had heard it in weeks, and I knew it meant something. I wondered if Christiaan heard it, too, or if it appeared only in my dreams. I had difficulty discerning my thoughts from my dreams in the night. I had the most wonderful dream. In it, Hannah visited me. We were both consumed by a golden light that surrounded us and ignited within us both. I asked her where she'd been, and she told me she had been on the most wonderful, glorious adventure. She apologized for leaving me behind, but she knew I would never go with her. She had been sad that I wouldn't go with her but happy that I would come with her now. We will have a splendid time, she tells me, a splendid time together as she shows me things I've never seen or imagined.

"Come along with me; follow me. Don't be afraid, Mama. Don't be afraid. It's going to be OK. I know the way. I know the way to joy, so much more than only fleeting happiness—a joy that I feel in my bones, a joy that took me to where I belong. I am home. I am the creator, the one to lead the way."

She was impatient for me to keep up. One foot forward, another foot planted behind—I was stuck in this spot.

"Come with me," she insisted.

She was so confident, so sure, so alive! I almost believed her. I wanted to believe her—I wanted to be her—to know, to be so sure, to be certain. Hannah lifted my face with her hands, and as she turned me toward yet another light, she breathed life into me, and I was overcome by an incredible sense of inner peace. As she breathed into me, I heard the lion's roar. It was the most wonderful of dreams. I desperately wanted her to stay with me, but she had to go, and this time I could not follow. When she left, I felt peaceful and strong and had a knowing that everything would turn out more than all right for both of us. I was certain I had heard the roar and that the roar had been real; it is a good omen when lions roar.

The dream made me realize it was time now for me to accept that Hannah may never return to me and that I would be OK, that I still had great things to do and to be in this life even without her by my side. I had not finished fulfilling my own divine path. The thought brought fresh tears to my eyes and deep in my soul, I knew this to be true. I was never "just" a wife. I was never "just" a mom. I was, and am, so much more than "just" anything.

My dearest Hannah,

You are so loved. You are love. I miss you. I miss you so terribly. I never thought I could experience such pain and loss and still be able to take a breath. I miss your laugh that cut through my sadness and brought me such joy; now, there is only silence. I miss the feel of your eyelashes as they brushed my cheek and flooded me with such a deep understanding of what love can be that I thought I might burst every single time you give me a butterfly kiss, but now there are no more kisses. I miss how you wriggled against my body to give and receive comfort, stirring every so often to ensure that I was still actually there—and now you aren't. I miss the way we'd each flare in anger in an instant, and then in the next, cajole each other in laughter with our silly faces and exaggerations. The only anger left is toward myself. I miss the sensation of your breath on my neck when your head was nestled between my shoulder and my ear, pushing deeper and deeper into my skin as if burrowing back inside, and now your breath has stopped. I miss catching your eye in the rearview mirror while driving you to school, your eyes locked with mine in an endless smile, your last smile now frozen on your lips. I miss your outrageous vocabulary and the way you would chatter on without contemplating the words you would use, never knowing just what your last words on Earth were. I miss the way you would stumble over your own feet and call out, "Nothing to see here!" That is what my whole heart is now calling out, "Nothing to see here!" I miss turning around and practically falling over you because that is how we moved, one never that far from the other. Now I trip on the emptiness all around me. I miss how at every age, your body fit perfectly with mine—two pieces that made a whole, and now I am much less than a half. I miss how the very first thing you did upon waking in the morning was to come find me and crawl into my lap, whether I was in my office, on the couch, or enjoying my coffee, but now my lap has no use, no cradle of solace for either one of us. I miss you playing hide and seek under a blanket or in a pile of pillows and pretending I couldn't find you, but now I am no longer pretending, and you are nowhere to be found.

You are an angel on Earth, the chosen one. To have you in my life, even for brief moments, were the best moments in my life. Thank you for choosing me, for saving me, for loving me.

I am the luckiest woman in the world to have had the experience of you. I love you with everything that I am—

—Mama

We still hadn't found Hannah or her body. The search had come to a halt, although Christiaan always took a different route each time he went out with a group of guests, and he looked in his spare time, sometimes taking me along. I had no idea how long I would remain, but there was no hurry. I knew in the depths of my soul that one day it would be time for Hannah to return to me, either in this life or the next.

I enjoyed the gift shop, and once Corlia gave birth, she, her husband, and their newborn baby boy moved back to his father's village. So, for now, the gift shop was mine to handle in almost any way I saw fit. I had come to love this little shop with its four walls. The shop was a blessing, and Akilah knew this when she asked me to fill in and ultimately take over the workings there. It wasn't the high-brow art gallery I was accustomed to, yet the artwork and crafts were even more amazing than anything I had encountered back home, and the speed here, or lack thereof, suited me just fine. I wasn't drinking anymore, and I found myself interested in things again. I asked Akilah if I could continue to help in the kitchen in the mornings before the camp awoke. And despite the protests of the other workers, she nodded yes. I came to love this too. The camaraderie between the women made me realize how much I had sacrificed in the way of my friendships when David came along. And I loved to cook when I had the time. The warmth and the aromas of the kitchen felt like home to me, felt like a real home. These activities provided me with a brief respite from my tortured thoughts and desperate hopes for Hannah.

I was rolling out the dough for the morning biscuits when I glanced up at the screen door in the back of the kitchen. The sun began to rise and shined brightly through the doorway. I looked up again, and yes, I did see it. There was a small silhouette of a girl. My brain registered she was too tall to be Behatti; it must be the child of a guest. I was hit with a deep sadness because I couldn't bear to hope that it might be my darling Hannah. I looked down at the dough before me, and I suddenly stopped dead. I knew it before I heard the voice.

"Mama, I'm home."

EPILOGUE

I AM ON A DIRT PATH covered in pea gravel. It is just a bit wider than me, surrounded by tall, lush, green grasses. I am not fighting to get through them, but they are lining the path, and I brush up against them as they wave in the wind. They are taller than me, but I can look up and see the brilliant blue sky above. The path winds gently and is mostly flat. As I look behind me, the path just kind of closes up as I go along. It is not scary; there is something vastly comforting here as I am half-walking, half-skipping, twirl-ing, jumping in an incredibly joyous state. I am perfectly happy to be on this path and full of excitement about where I am headed, even though I don't know where it is I am going. What I do know is that I am free; there are no tethers. All the burden, all the responsibilities are self-imposed. I am light. I am love. I am an exquisite being.

I realize my visions and dreams are God showing me all the truths about me, pointing me to my inner wisdom, my inner knowing. It is this voice I have come to trust, my own.

Darling Hannah and I are back in Denver. We stayed on at the camp for nearly a year. Hannah won't talk about what happened to her out there. I won't force her to tell me. It's her story, and she will tell it when and if she decides to. We have changed, she and I. When she returned to us, she was exhausted, weak, and thin. She was covered with substantial scratches, was filthy, and her hair was so matted and dirty that we had to clip most of it off.

But Hannah and I are fine; we are more than fine. No word from David. When we returned home, there was no sign of him—all his things cleared out some time ago, the divorce finalized. We moved into a townhouse near Hannah's school. We were both in agreement that we are meant to live a much simpler life. My heart was once attached to narrow ideals: my weight, my car, my job, my house. Now my heart is attached to the beauty that surrounds me, the unconditional love offered to me, the marvel of creation, and the pleasure of fulfillment. We both had been transformed by our adventures and our time in Africa. We fell in love with its people, its animals, and its landscape. We talk about moving there permanently some-day. But not right now. We are glad to be home, to be back among our familiar surroundings. Hannah is back at school with her friends and nearly no disruption. And I am making new friends. In essence, I am starting from scratch. No clear direction, per se, but I no longer feel lost in this big, vast world.

I am a lot less serious these days. I know now what true tragedy is—losing your daughter on a foreign continent, not the fact that the napkins don't match the paper plates. Or that an occasional Dum Dum wrapper gets left on the floor of the garage. I have found what makes me happy and continue to look for this pure, unadulterated kind of joy. I trust myself as I never have. I trust the decisions we are making in the way we choose to live our lives. Hannah is kind. She is courageous. She is smart. She is pure, unadul-terated love.

Now that we are home, we have a lot of quiet time, just

Hannah and me. I don't think of it as isolation; we just prefer our own company. We are both still healing and growing stronger in our own ways. I feel like a new woman who has been given yet another chance at this wondrous, amazing life. And my daughter is now back by my side to witness it and create her own.

We raise our glasses, smile at each other with a deep sense of love, and simultaneously say, "Here's looking at you, kid."

"Jinx, 1 2 3 4 5 6 7 8..."

"Stop!" I yell through my laughter.

Hannah crawls into my lap and cradles herself in my arms.

"I love you, Mama."

"I know, baby. I know, and I so love you too."

"We make each other better, don't we, Mama?"

"Yes, my love, we definitely make each other better."

Acknowledgments

THE THINGS I'VE LOVED the most about writing *When Lions Roar* are the amazing learning experiences and the incredible people I've met along the way who have helped to bring this creation to life. I now understand why authors' acknowledgments are a bit like an Oscar speech that has gone on for too long—cue the music.

I truly could not have done this alone. I have many people to thank and give appreciation to. My husband Jim who supported me in the background. Who took a chance when he married me; and together, created an amazing life that has allowed for extraordinary circumstances for this book to come to life. Thank you for your savvy business sense, your protection, and your love. Thank you for all the times you entertained our daughter, watched out for us, and singlehandedly did all the care and landscaping on the exterior of our home, making it the most beautiful and inspiring place on earth for me. Without you being the man you are, I would not be the woman I am today. I have grown and accomplished so much with you by my side, and am eternally grateful.

Thank you to our precious daughter, Jaymie, who so believes in me, there is no way I could let her down. Your generous, kind and loving spirit brings light to my life every single day. I love watching you develop into the woman that you will become. Life is markedly better with you in it.

My mentor, Rachael Jayne Groover, a woman I've known for many years who inspires me to walk my talk and be a better human every day. My publishing coach, Polly Letofsky, whose outrageous uplifting personality left me no room for doubt that I could do this. Victoria Wolf, the cover and layout designer, who really listened to me and created so many beautiful and compelling covers, it was difficult to choose. Friends and family who every time they saw me would ask how "the book" was coming along. I can't tell you how much that simple question fueled my spirit. Vanessa Tavernetti, my true soul sister, whose faith in me was unwavering and never let me forget how important it was to get this book out into the world.

Bobby Haas, my editor, a dream come true. His expertise and encouragement were more than I could have ever hoped for. He made this sometimes grueling process enjoyable and made me believe I had something very special to share.

The coaches I've worked with and those in my networking groups, thank you for holding space for me while I was undertaking this massive dream. Without your words of support, your wise ears for listening and your huge hearts for loving me, I never would have reached the finish line.

The country of South Africa, yes, the entire country. Its people, its landscape, and most of all its animals, the beautiful beasts. Getting to spend time with you profoundly changed my life and how I view the world. I returned to the States a deeply transformed woman for the better, and I thank you with my whole heart.

Gifting Back

WORKING ON THIS BOOK has been such an inspiration. It has always been a dream of mine to do more for the inhabitants of this planet, so a portion of the sale proceeds will go to the following nonprofit organizations whose work I deeply support.

ROAR FOUNDATION

The ROAR Foundation, a nonprofit organization based in Denver, Colorado, provides educational opportunities for women and girls who have suffered or are still experiencing sexual abuse and domestic violence. They provide training, education, counseling, mentorship, and other programs to help women and girls in crisis break the cycle of gender-based abuse and teach them to reclaim their sovereignty, identity, and voice so they are free to act in their own best interest.

To donate directly: www.roarfoundationusa.org

THE WILD ANIMAL SANCTUARY

This wildlife refuge is located in Keenesburg, Colorado, and its team travels across America and to countries around the world to rescue animals that are suffering. Each rescued animal is rehabilitated and released into large natural habitats with others of their kind. Their remarkable recoveries lead to lives filled with friendship, love, freedom, and joy!

To donate directly: www.wildanimalsanctuary.org

HERE'S HOW YOU CAN HELP.

Word of mouth is an author's most powerful marketing tool.

I encourage you to please:

- Write brilliant reviews at online book sites Amazon and Goodreads.
- Give copies of this book as gifts.

- Give the book a shout-out on your social media channels.
- Consider *When Lions Roar* for your book club and other group events.
- Be part of a movement! When you see a social media post about women's empowerment, add the hashtags #whenlionsroar and #roar.

Recommended
Resources

WHEN LIONS ROAR SALON
Book Discussion with the Author

For new readers of the book When Lions Roar, join author Karen Gruber one evening each month. Karen will read a short selection from her book and facilitate a lively discussion around one of the central themes from the novel. Participants will have the opportunity to ask questions of the author. Click or visit www.theinspiredmama.com/wlr-salon/ to register for the next upcoming conversation.

ROAR—THE EXPERIENCE℠

Trainings and Weekend Intensives

For the woman who is ready to reclaim her sovereignty, identity, and voice, this experience is designed to develop one's unique leadership style and presence. Participants will learn how to step into their feminine genius and dismantle any limiting and scarcity beliefs. This is a potent path to being fully expressed both personally and professionally and living your divine destiny. The first step is to email me at karen@theinspiredmama.com to request a time to chat about the suitability of the ROAR Experience℠ for you.

You can find out more about the ROAR Experience℠ here: www.theinspiredmama.com/roar-the-experience/

THE MASTERFUL MOM℠ SERIES

Private Mentorship

From recouping your identity, to regaining control of your life, to purposeful career development—if you are a mom, I've got you covered. The Masterful Mom℠ series is comprised of three separate tracks focused on specific solutions for moms based on where they are in life. Mentorship is a deeply personal and individualized opportunity. Contact me at karen@theinspiredmama.com to see which track is best for you and the life you are seeking.

Visit: www.theinspiredmama.com/work-with-me/

SPEAKING AND EXCLUSIVE AUTHOR ENGAGEMENTS

Conferences, Events, Keynotes

As a speaker, Karen is spirited, joyful, and unusually compelling with her courageous vulnerability. Her presentations equip and inspire audiences with practical solutions to effect change within themselves and the people around them. She supplies audiences with easy-to-master skills they can put to use right away in their professional and personal lives. Karen will personalize the ideal presentation based on audience needs.

Topics include:

- **Outsmart the Myth of Work + Life Balance:** How to become the authority of your life and powerfully lead yourself and your family.
- **Inspired Leader ~ Inspired Woman:** How to develop your unique leadership style and presence.
- **More Than a Mom:** How to embrace wellness as a path to personal leadership development.

For further inquiry, contact me at karen@theinspiredmama.com.

LET'S KEEP THE
CONVERSATION
GOING

NOW IT'S YOUR TURN. I invite you, yes you, to take a step into your leadership. There are many themes in this book that relate to being a mom and being a woman, and I am asking you to continue this conversation with your own circle of friends. We can't do life alone.

Although it is a work of fiction, a vast majority of this book was launched from real-life experiences, interviews, and conversations I have had with women and mothers over the past fifteen-plus years.

When Lions Roar is the perfect launchpad for starting these hard conversations that all too often get covered up with an "I'm fine," or "Everything's great." Be the vulnerable one to dig in with your friends, neighbors, fellow parishioners, and colleagues. This book is beneficial for groups whether they meet online or in person.

To make this easier for you, I have created a complimentary digital discussion guide. This guide includes thought-provoking questions sure to spark engaging discussions.

Visit www.theinspiredmama.com/wlr-book-club/ to download your FREE digital discussion guide.

About the
Author

KAREN GRUBER is an international #1 best-selling contributing author, inspirational speaker, and a Leadership Development Coach for women and moms. She specializes in inspiring moms to realize their potential as mothers, women, and leaders.

Karen has had extensive specialized training in parenting, feminine spirituality, and leadership. Over the past fifteen years, she has provided innovative leadership coaching for moms and has dramatically transformed her own life.

Her greatest joys are sharing her life with her husband, Jim, and daughter, Jaymie, presenting her message to women, and traveling the world.

She is the founder of *The Inspired Mama,* a company located in gorgeous Denver, Colorado, that focuses on the inspiration, leadership, and well-being of women and moms.

When Lions Roar is Karen's debut fictional work. As for hobbies, she is freakish about Christmas lights and loves to play Baccarat.

To book Karen for speaking, book clubs, or coaching opportunities, contact her at karen@theinspiredmama.com.